FIENDS AND FESTIVALS

Related titles by S. Usher Evans

PRINCESS VIGILANTE
The City of Veils
The Veil of Ashes
The Veil of Trust
The Queen of Veils

THE SEOD CROÍ CHRONICLES
A Quest of Blood and Stone
A Quest of Earth and Magic
A Quest of Sea and Soil
A Quest of Aether and Dust

THE MADION WAR TRILOGY
The Island
The Chasm
The Union

FIENDS AND FESTIVALS

Weary Dragon Inn

BOOK TWO

S. Usher Evans

Sun's Golden Ray
Publishing

Pensacola, FL

Version Date: 7/30/23
© 2023 S. Usher Evans
ISBN: 978-1945438608

Map created by Luke Beaber of Stardust Book Services
Line Editing by Danielle Fine, By Definition Editing

Sun's Golden Ray Publishing
Pensacola, FL
www.sgr-pub.com

For ordering information, please visit
www.sgr-pub.com/orders

In loving memory

Mr. L. Biscuit

2008-2022

Town Hall

Witzel Butchery

Weary Dragon Inn

Town Square

Library

Mackey Bakery

Pigsend Tea Shop

ool

Flour Mill

Pigsend Village

CHAPTER ONE

"A little higher on the left, I think."

Bev pulled the rope tighter, and the Pigsend Harvest Festival banner rose an inch. On the other side, Vellora Witzel held the other rope steady. The blonde, broad-shouldered butcher turned to her wife, Ida, who was ten paces away, surveying the banner with a scrutinizing gaze.

"Well?" Vellora said with an impatient sigh.

"Maybe a little higher?" Ida said.

"Why don't you come hold it, then?" Vellora huffed. "We've been standing here for half an hour while you dither with it."

Whereas Vellora was tall and muscular, her wife

was small, lithe, with tawny skin and black, coiled hair that had been pulled in a tight bun today. Even with their size differences, they were a perfect match, glaring at each other with equal annoyance.

Bev cleared her throat to break the tension. "Ida?"

"Fine." She threw her hands in the air. "It's as good as it's gonna get, I suppose. I want everything to be perfect."

"It will be," Bev said with an affirming smile as she tied the rope to a stake in the ground. "Because you're in charge."

Ida gave Bev a look. She was the chair of the Harvest Festival Committee this year, and for the past two weeks, had been scurrying around like one of Rosie Kelooke's demon chickens to make sure the seven-day festival would run smoothly. It was the biggest and most anticipated event of the year in Pigsend, filled with competitions, vendors, and all sorts of activities—and brought in a ton of people and business for the economy of Pigsend before things all but shut down for the winter.

"Well, if that's all," Vellora said, sounding a bit less annoyed. "One of us has to mind the shop, you know. Can't spend all day here."

Ida rolled her eyes. "I haven't asked you to do *that* much. Just hang the banner in the square, help us set up the tents and barns for the judging—"

"Reserve two rooms for the festival judges," Bev said with an easy smile.

"Well? Consider it easy money," Ida said.

"Yes, but I'd already had bookings. Had to tell a heartbroken Lazlo Murtagh that his cousin would have to stay with him this year," Bev said with a snicker. "I've never seen a person so distraught."

"Family can be tough," Vellora said.

"Wouldn't know." Bev chuckled as she glanced at the clock atop the nearby town hall. "I do, however, have a few things in the oven I need to tend to, so I must be getting back. Ida, if you need anything else, you know where to find me."

"Yeah, yeah," Ida said, gently resting her hand on Vellora's stomach. "Thanks, Bev."

Bev whistled as she walked the short distance back to her beloved Weary Dragon Inn. It was a quaint building, two stories tall, with white plaster walls and a thatched roof. It was the only inn in town, and with the expected influx of farmers, tradesmen, and others eager to compete in the many different contests held during the festival, Bev was already knee-deep in preparations. Her vegetable stores were overflowing, as was her flour and other baking supplies. The inn had never been cleaner, especially with a fresh coat of paint and a brand-new front wall.

The dirt near the entrance was still a slightly

different color than the rest of the road, filled in after a sinkhole threatened to swallow the whole building. Bev couldn't help but notice it every time she passed by, opting to walk through the kitchen instead. She wasn't superstitious—and there hadn't been another earthquake or sinkhole since they'd discovered the queen's soldiers disrupting a hidden magical river—but she didn't want to push her luck so close to the biggest week of the year.

Sin, Bev's trusty old mule, was enjoying the cool fall day and brayed when Bev approached. The mule had once had a mean reputation, hence her full name *Sinister*, but she'd mellowed out in her old age.

"Are you excited about the festival, too?" Bev asked. "Or are you looking for a carrot?"

The mule brayed again.

"Sorry, girl. Need to save them for the paying customers." Bev patted her on the nose. "But once they're all gone, I'll be sure to give you the leftovers."

Bev left the mule there and went to inspect her small herb garden. The rosemary plant was big and fragrant, the thyme and basil swaying in the wind. The former would last the winter, of course, but as soon as the weather got colder, Bev would need to move the more delicate herbs inside to a pot on her windowsill. She plucked a few more sprigs of rosemary to dry for her famous bread—if history was any indication, the dining room would be full of people looking for it.

With the sprigs in hand, she rose and turned—and nearly fell into her garden. "Oh! Allen, I didn't hear you walk up."

The young baker from across the street was looking much happier and less prickly these days, especially now that his bakery was making the tidy profit needed to keep it afloat. "Saw you come back," he said, lifting the basket of muffins. "Today's haul."

"I told you your debt's been repaid," Bev said, crossing the yard to stand next to him. "You don't need to keep bringing me these delectable muffins." She took a sniff. "What are they, blueberry?"

He nodded. "With a pinch of cinnamon."

Bev should've sent him on his way, but she couldn't help plucking a muffin off the top. "This really isn't necessary," she said, promising herself she'd only take *one*.

"I still owe you at least two gold pieces," he said, his cheeks growing dark with a blush. "And Mama would come back and haunt me if I left a debt unpaid, especially after all you did for me."

Bev shook her head. "It was nothing. And you helped me, too."

"I insist."

"Well, then *I* insist you hold on to these favors until my inn is full of people," Bev said, taking a second muffin despite her earlier promise and eating it in two bites. "Are you still not using the…uh…help?"

He shook his head proudly. "No, this is all me."

Bev beamed. Allen had been sneaking to the dark forest north of town to buy magic from a magical creature called a barus to recreate his mother's recipes, and Bev had managed to convince the creature (through a great deal of gold) to give him the magic his mother had possessed. Instead of using it, though, Allen had been hard at work perfecting his own recipes. And Bev couldn't have been prouder.

"Well, you're doing great. But you'd better take that basket back to your shop before I turn into a blueberry myself." She chuckled. "You hear?"

"I hear, I hear." He took a step back. "Are you planning on entering the bread competition this year?"

"Absolutely not," Bev said with a chuckle. "Wouldn't be fair to the other contestants, you know?"

Allen grinned. "Perhaps not. But it would be nice to see that blue ribbon stay in Pigsend for once instead of going elsewhere."

"We have plenty of ribbons," Bev said. "Herman

Monday always wins the gourd competition."

"Unless Trent has anything to say about it."

Bev smiled; the two farmers had gone to great lengths to try to outdo each other in the gourd competition. "We'll see."

"Well, I guess I'd better get back to it," Allen said. "If you're sure you don't want more—"

"Okay, one more." Bev plucked another muffin off the pile. "You're a devil, Allen."

He beamed.

Full of sugar and berries, Bev returned to the kitchen and checked the pot inside the oven. A large piece of fatty beef was cooking in a bath of red wine and aromatics, but it would need a few hours yet until it was fall-off-the-bone tender. Near the oven was a mixing bowl covered in a kitchen towel, which Bev lifted to inspect the rise on her latest batch of rosemary bread. The earthy scent was intoxicating and welcoming, but it needed a bit more time. Still, it would pair well with the beef stew she was planning to serve this evening.

Most nights, Bev served dinner to anyone who walked in the door of the Weary Dragon Inn. Of course, overnight guests' meals were included in their room price, but those who weren't staying paid half a silver. Since Bev had started making her famous rosemary bread again, the number of diners had swelled from four or five to at least ten. It was good money to sock away for the upcoming quiet months—especially after having to make repairs to the inn.

While Bev would've certainly preferred her inn to stay in one piece, the upside to the renovations were that the place was a bit more *hers* now. There was new paneling in the dining room, a dark mahogany better suited to the color of the three tables. The front door, too, had been carved just a bit differently and painted a forest green. A vase, courtesy of the local artist Ramone Comely, sat on a nice table in the corner. She'd always loved this place—the first in her short memory that she'd called home—but now it was extra special. Wim McKee, the old innkeeper who'd left the inn to her, would've been proud.

She'd gotten in the habit of taking most of her cues from her late boss, including not entering the Harvest Festival bread-making contest. He'd said it was unfair to enter such an obviously award-winning loaf and sweep the competition every year. But Allen's words sat on her shoulders, tempting her to do something *else* differently and claim it as her own.

Baking another loaf for the contest wouldn't be much more work than she was already doing. She would need a preliminary taste for the initial round then another entry on competition day. Since she was already planning on making at least five loaves a day...

Don't do it, old girl. Wim's voice was clear in her mind.

Glancing at the clock on the mantel above the fireplace, she decided she'd give the bread another thirty minutes or so before kneading it and putting it into loaf pans. With the kitchen chores done, she headed out to the front hall to sit and wait for any customers who might have traveled a day early to town.

It was cool, but not quite cold enough to light the fire in the hearth, so she settled on her usual perch behind the front desk. There, she kept her keys, ledger, and anything else her guests might need. She'd just sat down on her stool when the door opened, and a young man Bev hadn't seen before came walking in, looking bewildered with a bag slung around his shoulders.

"Good afternoon. This is the local inn, is it not?" He checked a scrap of paper in his hand. "The Weary Dragon?"

Bev nodded. "It is. Welcome to Pigsend."

He brightened and scurried over to the front desk. "My name is Claude Bonding. I'm here to judge the Harvest Festival Competitions."

Bev frowned as she opened her ledger. She

didn't have him on her list of room reservations. "Oh dear, there must've been some mix-up. I don't have a room reserved for you."

"Do you have one for Alice Winter?" he asked, peering down. "Ah, there she is. Unfortunately, Ms. Winter has come down with a bad cold and was unable to make the journey. I'm her nephew. She sent me in her stead."

"Oh, well that's a shame. Ms. Winter was always a lovely guest," Bev said. "I hope she makes a full recovery."

"She's not the youngest girl, but she'll be fine, I'm sure." He had a warm smile that put Bev at ease. "I can assure you I'm quite up to the task of filling her shoes. I spent most of my childhood by her side in the kitchen. She was like a second mom to me."

"Well, we appreciate you stepping in to help in her time of need," Bev said, pulling the room key. "The Harvest Festival Committee has already paid for your room, so here is your key. Dinner will be around sundown tonight. It'll be beef stew and rosemary bread—"

"Oh, *the* rosemary bread?" Claude's face lit up in excitement. "I've heard so much about it."

"I hope it lives up to your expectations," she said, sliding his key over to him. "My name's Bev, by the way. If you need anything at all, please don't hesitate to ask. I'm usually downstairs or in the kitchen, and I'm happy to help. Do you have any bags I can carry upstairs for you?"

"Just the one, and I can manage," he said, taking the key. "I might need some directions to the town square tomorrow, though."

"Take this road out front toward the right," Bev said. "I just finished hanging a big sign, and the square's full of vendor tents and activity. You can't miss it!"

"Thanks!"

The young judge had a small sack slung over his shoulder as he eagerly climbed the stairwell to the second floor. Bev listened for the sound of his door closing before she struck through *Alice Winter* on the ledger and wrote *Claude Bonding* right above. Ida hadn't mentioned anything about switching judges, but with the flurry of activity that went into the final day before the festival was to begin, it must've slipped through the cracks.

She closed her book and readied herself to greet the rest of her guests.

That evening, Claude was the first in line to serve himself dinner. He was joined by Bardoff Boyd, the local schoolteacher, Earl Dollman, the carpenter, and Etheldra Daws, who owned the tea shop down the road. Then Max Sterling, the librarian, and the Brewer twins, Stella and Shasta, joined them. Before too long, the entire pot of beef stew was gone, and the rosemary loaf was nothing but crumbs.

"I have to say, that lived up to all my expectations," Claude said, patting his stomach. "Tell me you'll be entering the competition."

"Bev's too stingy," Etheldra said.

"I'm not stingy." Bev collected their empty bowls and plates. "I happen to think it's unfair to enter."

"And why's that?" Claude asked with a cheery grin.

"Because, obviously, I'd win," she said, earning her a few chuckles from those seated.

"I don't know. I hear Lazlo's cousin is bringing her legendary rye," Earl replied. "I saw her today at his house."

Bev winced. "I do hope there's no bad blood there. I had to cancel her reservation to make room for the judges."

"They'll survive," Earl said, rising slowly. "It's only a week."

"Not that I'm allowed to say anything," Claude said, gesturing to the bread. "But I do think you should enter. I don't know if it would win, as I haven't tasted any of the other entries, but I do think it's worthy of an award."

Bev smiled. "I'll think about it. I'll be making

another batch tomorrow anyway, so I could—"

"Oh, you should!" Shasta said, clapping her hands. "Imagine what it would be like to have that blue ribbon hanging from your mantel in here."

"And you deserve all the awards after solving the sinkhole problem," Stella added. "Oh, Bev. You really should enter."

A rousing "*hear, hear*" came from the rest of the group.

Bev's cheeks warmed. "I didn't do anything really—"

"What sinkhole problem?" Claude asked.

"About a month ago, we started getting earthquakes and sinkholes in town," Shasta said. "Took our house out, and nearly took out the inn here. But Bev managed to figure out it was the dastardly—"

Stella put her hand over her twin's, perhaps to remind her they were in mixed company. "The queen's soldiers had inadvertently caused them."

"Oh, goodness. I'm sure they were quite apologetic," Claude said.

Bev ducked into the kitchen with the dirty bowls to hide her expression as the crowd answered his question with a chorus of colorful descriptions. Apologetic, they surely were not—in fact, they'd threatened to come back and raze the town. But so far, they hadn't seen hide nor hair of them.

When she returned, the diners had continued the story and had gotten to the part about the town trial.

"A mole man!" Claude said. "Such a thing exists?"

"He's entering the fiber arts contest, isn't he?" Earl said. "He's a master knitter."

"I believe so," Bev said with a nod. She'd made it out to see Merv once since the town meeting where he'd almost been arrested by the queen's soldiers, and she'd finally been able to convince him to enter one of his beautiful blankets, but only if she came to retrieve his entry and hung around for a cup of tea.

"The town sure is lucky to have a super sleuth like you around," Claude said to Bev. "And a master baker, too. What else can you do?"

"I'm just a simple innkeeper," Bev said. "I wake up, make bread, keep things tidy. Nothing special about me at all."

"Except we have no clue who you were before you showed up in town," Etheldra said with a raised brow.

"Oh?" Claude turned. "Is that so?"

Etheldra nodded and continued with her usual, pointed tone. "She showed up here, stumbling around with no name, no family, no skills."

Bev chuckled. "You're too nice, Etheldra."

"And how'd you come to be here at the inn?" Claude asked.

"The old innkeeper gave me a job as a beverage wench," she said.

"Is that..." Claude laughed nervously. "Is that why you're called—"

"Bev? Absolutely." She grinned. "Anyway, I've been working here these past five years. Couldn't ask for a better life."

"You don't miss anything about your old one?" Claude asked.

"Can't remember anything to miss."

"Not even a little?"

Bev started, recalling the few moments of clarity when she was investigating the sinkholes. And that... No, she wouldn't think about what was buried in her garden. She was doing her best to forget it.

"Not even a little," she said. "Now if you lot are finished, I've got to get in the back to clean up. Expecting a full house tomorrow, so I want to be prepared." She nodded to Claude. "If you need anything at all, I'm down the hall."

CHAPTER TWO

The first day of the Harvest Festival dawned bright and crisp, with nary a cloud in the sky. Bev was able to get through her morning chores quickly, as she'd done the lion's share the night before. She walked out into the main hall where Allen had left a basket of muffins. They looked and smelled like apple cinnamon today.

"Allen, you devil," she said, snatching one and taking a bite.

"Oh, good morning!" Claude popped up from one of the two armchairs in front of the fireplace. "I wasn't sure if those muffins were for…"

"Patrons of the inn," Bev said. "But be warned,

they're addicting."

He took one bite, and a guttural moan came from his lips. "You aren't kidding."

"Come on," Bev said with a chuckle. "I'll walk with you to the town square. Otherwise, we'll sit here and eat this entire basket before noon."

Claude was as friendly today as the night before, asking all sorts of questions about the town and the shops as they passed. Bev pegged him about mid-thirties, but he had a youthful air to him and an inquisitiveness that was refreshing. He seemed to want to know everything about everyone, which Bev was more than happy to provide.

"I'll be sure to steer clear of the chickens, then," he said as they passed under the banner Bev had hung the day before. The town square had been transformed in the hours since, with big white tents taking up every corner of the space.

There was a growing crowd as well, with more unfamiliar faces than Bev had seen the day before. Most folks were within a day's ride of town, so they'd get up early and go home late. Others were staying with friends and relatives in town, and some entrepreneurial residents of Pigsend had offered spare bedrooms to rent. Bev didn't mind the competition. The more people in Pigsend, the more money flowing to the coffers of the local businesses. And her dining room would be packed regardless.

The bulk of the contests would be held inside Pigsend Town Hall. A large sign out front listed the schedule of events, starting this morning with the opening ceremony. Ida was rushing around the front steps, talking with this person and that, directing traffic and decorations.

She beamed when she saw Bev. "Bev! Hi..." Ida blinked. "Who are you?"

"Claude Bonding," he said, holding out his hand. "My aunt Alice couldn't make it to judge this year, so she sent me in her place."

"Oh, goodness," Ida said. "I'm so sorry to hear that. Is she all right?"

"Perfectly fine," he said. "Just a cold. At her age, she didn't want to travel. You know how that goes. But I promise, she's taught me well, and I'm eager to see what the festival has to offer."

"Excellent. Our other judge is right over here," Ida said, gesturing to a short, squat lady with beady eyes and a permanent frown. "Petula Banks. She's just arrived in town and hasn't yet checked in to the inn. Petula, this is Claude Bonding, who'll be judging with you, and Bev...uh. Just Bev. She's the innkeeper at the Weary Dragon."

"Pleased to meet you," Bev said, holding out her hand. "It's rare we get two new judges for the festival. Where are you from, Petula?"

"Queen's Capital," she said with a look. "As part

of Her Majesty's official judging corps."

Ida shifted uncomfortably, and Bev could almost feel her relief that Vellora wasn't around. Ida's wife had been in the war five years ago, fighting on the losing Kingside. Any mention of Queen Meandra ruffled her feathers, and the presence of her soldiers was just as bad. Unfortunately, Bev counted two in the queen's service standing at attention behind Petula.

"Those are...new," she said. "What are they doing here?"

"Petula brought them," Ida said, forcing herself to look neutral. "Apparently, it's standard for an entourage of soldiers to accompany a member of the...what was your job again, Petula, dear?"

"Her Majesty's Official Judging Corps." She flashed a shiny pin.

"I wasn't aware there was such a thing," Bev said, looking at Ida. "Is it new?"

Petula nodded. "Part of a new initiative by Queen Meandra to bring some...shall we say *process rigor* around the enterprise of these local festival competitions. Her Majesty felt it prudent to outline a standard set of justifications for each of the different competitions to ensure a fair and balanced contest. You can find it all in this book." She snapped her fingers, and one of the soldiers walked over carrying a thick, leather-bound book bearing the inscription, *The Official Criteria for Agrarian-based Competitions, Volume I.*

"I'd hate to see Volume II," Ida muttered so low only Bev could hear.

"Well, that sounds...reasonable," Claude said with a weak smile. "Aunt Alice never said anything about any criteria, but if I could borrow a copy, I'm sure I could read up on what I need to know."

"Oh, don't worry about it." Petula's small lips formed a patronizing smile. "I'm well-versed in the numbers. I'm sure you're here for...well, a *second* opinion."

Claude glanced at Ida, who glanced at Bev, and there was a long pause between the four of them.

"Well, I suppose we should be getting on with the opening ceremonies," Ida said, with a nervous laugh. "Petula, Claude, if you'll follow me, I'll lead you to the stage. I'm sure the crowd's already gathered. Bev...see you around?"

"Indeed. I've got to get back to the inn," Bev said with a nod. "Petula, whenever you'd like to check in, your room's ready."

Petula didn't even look back as she walked into the town hall building.

Bev glanced at the soldiers, checking to see if any of them belonged to the troublesome quintet who'd caused the sinkholes. But where those soldiers had been stoic, focused, and given off an air of superiority, these seemed to be a bit more…for lack of a better word, relaxed. They slouched a bit, wearing no weapons, and their tunics were rumpled. And to boot, they smiled at Bev when they caught her gaze.

"So where are you fine folks staying?" Bev asked. "I'd offer to put you up at the inn, but we're booked up. I don't think you'd fancy sleeping with my mule Sin out in the barn, either."

The first soldier chuckled affably. "Don't worry about us. We'll be traveling in from nearby Middleburg."

"Oh, wow…" Bev said with raised brows. "That's pretty far from your charge."

"About an hour or so on the horses. Not too bad. But our primary job was to escort her here and back to Queen's Capital safely."

"And we get to enjoy the festival, too," said the second before putting his hand on his chest. "My name's Marcelano, by the way. This is Ridge."

"Bev," she said with a nod. "Is this a regular job of yours, attending these festivals?"

"Oh, for sure. We've been on the go nonstop for about six months," Ridge said with a nod, patting his stomach. "Best job I've ever had, I'll tell you. Probably should lay off the pies, though."

"You two are welcome to dinner at the Weary Dragon tonight," Bev said. "And if I happen to get a room cancellation, I'll be sure to let you know." She turned to leave. "Enjoy the festival, and welcome to Pigsend!"

Ida's voice echoed from the stage beyond as Bev headed away from the crowd. The welcome ceremony was more or less the same every year, and Bev really did need to be getting back. When she passed the Witzel Butcher Shop, Vellora waved with a nice smile, so perhaps Ida *hadn't* told her wife about the soldiers—and Bev wasn't going to be the one to break the news, so she waved back and quickly scurried into the inn.

The front room was empty, so she propped the kitchen door open to hear anyone coming in and set to work preparing dinner. First, the rosemary bread.

With care, she pulled a small jar from the corner. It was a mixture of warm water, dough from the day before, honey, and fresh barm—yeast Bev pulled off the top of the beer she served with dinner. The concoction gave off a delicious scent and bubbles had appeared on the top, signaling it was active and ready for the day's baking.

On her large kitchen table, Bev carefully measured out flour and a little salt into her extra large mixing bowl and created a well in the center, where she poured a bit of the starter. She mixed in flour, creating a ball of dough and leaving it there for the moment.

Crossing the kitchen to the window, she grabbed a bunch of rosemary hanging from the sill. It smelled amazing, even before she did anything with it. Although the small, long leaves weren't big, chopping them before incorporating them into the bread enhanced the flavor much more than the way Wim had taught her. So she ran her fingers along the wooden stems, releasing the leaves to the cutting board. Then, with her large kitchen knife, she roughly chopped and added them to the dough, mixing them in until perfectly blended. A tea towel went on top of the bowl as-is, and the dough went to a warm spot near the oven to proof.

For the next few hours, she peeled potatoes and carrots, put in an order with Vellora for some pork (making sure *not* to mention the soldiers), and when she came back and lifted the tea towel, the dough had doubled in size.

"Perfect," she said with a smile.

She turned the mixing bowl over and dumped the sticky dough onto the counter. Then, she started the arduous process of kneading the dough, adding more flour until it reached the right consistency. It transformed into a stretchy ball with flecks of rosemary mixed evenly throughout.

She plucked her knife off the kitchen table and oiled it with some lard. But she hesitated as she stood over the ball.

She could cut it into fifths—that was what the recipe called for. And that was what she usually did. Five loaves would be enough for this evening for sure.

But…the conversation from the night before rang in her head. Hanging the blue ribbon over the mantel *would* be nice, especially after all the chaos from the sinkholes. And Bev had made a few tweaks to the recipe over the years, not just the yeast, but the amount of barm she got from the casks of beer —and the beer itself was a bit different from when Wim had brewed it.

"Oh, don't be silly," Bev said to herself, looking up at nothing. "You shouldn't enter this contest. It'd be for your ego, and nothing else."

"And why shouldn't you give in to that ego of yours?" A dark-haired, pale woman with ruby red lips swept into the kitchen from the front door. Mayor Jo Hendry, dressed impeccably in a dark jacket and pants, smiled at Bev. "You deserve to be celebrated."

Bev brushed her forehead with the back of her flour-covered hands. "Mayor Hendry, to what do I owe the pleasure?"

"Just thought I'd pop in to see how our favorite innkeeper is doing," she said almost too brightly. "Fully booked? No cancellations?"

"As of right now, one adjustment," Bev said, explaining Claude's swap with his aunt briefly. "But I assume you've met him if you were down at the welcome ceremony."

"I did." So that wasn't the real reason for her appearance. "And I see our other judge came with some friends, too."

"Mm." Bev nodded. "Seem real friendly. Unlike the last crew."

"And that's what I want to talk with you about," Hendry said. "I know we've had some trouble with *select* members of the queen's service in the past. I hope you'll treat our new guests with the usual amount of...grace and kindness."

Bev was quick to offer a comforting grin. "Of course. I already had a nice chat with them about where they were staying. Seem like a pleasant group of folks. As long as they aren't diverting any magical rivers—"

"And I *also* think we should keep any mention of the events of the last month under wraps," Hendry continued, cutting her off harshly. "You know, just to keep the light on the town positive. We always have those from Middleburg and elsewhere who think our town is too small to house a *proper* festival."

"They're welcome to host their own, of course," Bev said, turning back to the boule and sprinkling a bit more flour onto it. "No rule saying they can't."

"Ah, that's where you're wrong. There *are* rules now. And…" She shifted uncomfortably. "I believe that's why Ms. Petula Banks is here. I fear she's inspecting how we run our festival. If the next week doesn't go flawlessly, she could, by rights, shut down the festival. Permanently. I don't think I have to tell you what that would mean for the town's economy."

Bev nodded. "We mentioned it to Claude, but I'll keep mum from here on out. I think people will be too wrapped up in all the competitions to notice."

"And *speaking* of competitions," Hendry's gaze dropped to the large dough ball, "are you planning on entering the bread-making competition this year?"

"Considering it," Bev said. "Just don't know if it's fair."

"Why wouldn't it be? You make this bread. You've got as much right as anyone else to make your claim to the blue ribbon." She tilted her head. "Unless you don't think yourself worthy of praise?"

Bev adjusted the knife on the table. "Just don't usually seek out attention, you know? That business with the sinkholes is the last time I want to be hauled up in front of a town meeting ever again." She caught Hendry's gaze. "My sneaking-around days are *over*."

"I'm just saying…" Hendry said, running her finger along the edge of the table. "It might be yet another feather in Pigsend's cap if we were to bring home top prizes in *all* the categories. Between Herman and Trent, we're a shoo-in for the gourd competition. Freddie Silver's pigs are a good contender, as are Bathilda Wormwood's cows. We've got some excellent submissions for the fiber arts competition, the jams, the pies…" She rattled off other contests, naming a citizen of Pigsend as a potential winner for each. "The only thing we *don't* have is a good entry into the bread-making competition. In fact, everyone entering is from out of town."

The mayor smiled, and there was a tickle of something in the back of Bev's mind, almost as if the mayor's words were laced with *magic*. Bev never pried into people's history, and now, knowing there were representatives of Queen Meandra in town, it was important to keep those kinds of questions to herself. But she'd suspected their mayor might have been elected through more than her winning smile and impeccable lip color.

"I'll think about it," Bev said.

"Please do. As a personal favor to me." Hendry's gaze fell to the dough by Bev's hand. "You won't need much for the sample loaf, you know. Just a fist-sized amount. I'm sure you can spare it."

"When the denizens of the Weary Dragon Inn complain that I've run out of bread, I'll be sure to point them to your door," she said.

"Do that." Hendry winked as she stepped away. "Have a good day, Bev."

Within seconds, she was gone, leaving only the echo of their conversation in Bev's mind. It was a lot to think about, and the last thing Bev wanted was to draw attention to herself, even in the pursuit of culinary greatness. But as she caught her reflection in the knife in her hand, she considered maybe… maybe this once she could take a little for herself.

She sliced the dough into sixths, putting each into a lard-coated pan, and set them, covered in a tea towel, in the warm spot near the oven to proof again until ready to bake.

CHAPTER THREE

As predicted, the inn's large tavern was packed with dinner guests, and Bev barely had enough to feed everyone. The rosemary bread was gone within minutes, with half the guests not getting any (and complaining loudly). Etheldra Daws was beside herself with fury that she'd missed out, and demanded Bev go into the back and bake her another loaf.

"Sorry, dear," Bev said, holding up her hands, "these things take time."

That wasn't entirely true. There *was* a fully baked sixth loaf sitting under a tea towel on her kitchen table. Bev could've broken it out and shared it with the angry customers, though there were far too many of them to slice it equitably. But she held her tongue.

After the crowd dissipated, the dishes were cleaned, and the floor swept, Bev retired to her room to dream about herself winning the coveted blue ribbon. When sunrise came, Bev washed up and dressed quickly, intent on sprinting through her morning chores and heading down to the festival first thing. She descended the stairs and found another basket of muffins on the counter—this time pumpkin or perhaps sweet potato.

Bev walked by it, telling herself she would *not* be eating another one of Allen's muffins today. And yet, she couldn't help herself as she turned and plucked one off the top to munch on while she tended to—

She stopped short.

The kitchen towel was there. But the loaf was gone.

Slowly, she lowered the muffin from her lips, the taste disappearing on her tongue. She *had* left the bread right here on the clean kitchen table, covered in a tea towel, ready to be delivered...right? She licked her lips and replayed the night before, recalling every one of her guests walking up to their room. Of course, the back door was unlocked so someone could've swept in and taken it...

But for what purpose?

The bread was delicious, of course. Maybe someone had enjoyed a bit too much of Bev's ale and come in looking for a snack. There were a thousand different explanations for what might've happened.

Bev glanced at the clock. It was early still. She had plenty of flour and ingredients left. There was barm starter ready for today's baking. If she got going now, she could get everything together and in the oven and *just barely* make the entry deadline by five o'clock this afternoon.

To be sure, she searched the entire kitchen for evidence of the bread. But it was truly and totally gone.

"Good thing I spiffed up yesterday," she muttered, grabbing her starter and getting to work.

Two hours later, she had another rising loaf near the oven, though it was still chilly, and it would take longer to rise than usual. To speed things along, she went to start a fire, but found the one thing she'd forgotten to refill in her mad dash to get the inn ready was firewood.

"Shoot." Hand to her head, she walked through the inn and peered out the front door. Allen's light was on—bakers did get up early—so she quickly crossed the street and rapped on his back door.

"Bev?" He opened the door wider. "What can I do for you? Was there a problem with the muffins?"

"Oh, heavens, no," she said. "You didn't... You didn't see anything out of the ordinary at the inn when you were dropping them off, did you?"

He frowned. "In what way?"

She explained the missing loaf. "And I'll be darned if I know... It seems so random. Who would steal a loaf of bread?"

"Maybe someone found out you were entering," Allen said with an affable smile. Before Bev could ask, he explained, "Mayor Hendry came by yesterday to ask if I'd enter the bread-making competition. You know bread was never our specialty, so I told her she should be across the street talking with you."

Bev blew air between her lips. "Well, in any case, if I do want to bring glory and prestige to our town, I need to warm up my kitchen and wouldn't you know it? I'm all out of firewood. Would you mind if I—"

"Of course not!" He jumped away from the door and rushed toward his own hearth, which was overflowing with wood. He gathered three or four logs into his arms and brought them over. "Anything for you."

"Thanks, Allen. I suppose I'll have to carve out time to get some more today. Whenever that'll be."

"I should be wrapping up here soon," he said. "I'd be happy to get you some firewood. I hear Dane Sterling has a big pile from a tree he chopped down a few months ago. Real good stuff."

"I think I should be able to manage," she said. "And maybe I can get some more flour from Sonny while I'm over that way. With the way these folks are going through my bread, I'll probably need to quadruple my recipe to make everyone happy."

Allen beamed. "Well, let me know how I can help."

"This is great, Allen. You're a star."

Bev got a small fire going in the kitchen and busied herself with other tasks while she waited for the temperature in the room to rise. She checked on the dough a few times and was pleased to see it finally spring to life with the warmer temperature. Then she put up a sign at the front desk promising she'd be back within an hour or so and headed out back to get Sin ready to go.

"Gotta get some supplies, old girl," Bev said, handing the mule a carrot. "If you don't mind."

The mule chomped happily, allowing herself to be hooked onto Bev's cart, and soon they were on their way toward the eastern side of town. Bev couldn't have moved the mule faster for anything, but she still tried coaxing her to a faster pace than usual.

"Not trying to be mean, girl," Bev explained. "But we do have a lot to get done today and not a lot of time to be doing it."

They reached Dane's property, where there was a huge stack of firewood near the side of the road. The farmer was nearby, tending to their goats, and turned to wave at Bev.

"Beautiful morning, eh, Bev? Need some wood?"

"The only thing I forgot," she said with a smile as she hopped off the wagon to help herself. "We've had some nice weather lately, so it must've slipped my mind."

The farmer glanced at the sky. "Might want to double up. I feel there's gonna be a storm coming soon. Weather's changing."

"Let's hope it holds off until the festival's over," Bev said, picking up a few pieces of wood and tossing them in the back of the wagon. "Ida would be devastated if all the hard work we put in to set up those tents went to waste."

He chuckled and hopped the fence to help Bev. "I hear you're thinking about entering the bread-making competition!"

"Boy, news does travel fast in a small town," Bev said, trying to hide her annoyance. "Darnedest thing. I had a loaf ready to submit last night. This morning, it was gone." She shrugged. "Hoping I can make another as good before the cutoff tonight."

"Oh, I doubt you'll have any problem with that," he said. "But that is fascinating. Maybe someone's out to sabotage you?"

Bev would've dismissed him, laughing it off as ridiculous, but the Harvest Festival brought out the worst in people, especially those who put great stock in the number of ribbons they won. "Don't know any of the other competitors, really. All I know is they're all from out of town. That's why I'm entering. Mayor Hendry...uh..." Bev laughed, unsure if she should say. "Well, let's just say she asked me to try to keep the prize local this year."

"I say, good for her. We all know that bread of yours is award-winning. Might as well get the ribbon for it."

Bev smiled as she put another piece in. "That should last me a bit, I hope. This is some good-looking wood." She reached into her pocket and pulled out a silver. "Thanks—"

"Oh, it's on me, I insist." He held up his hands. "If it's going toward that bread, it's a worthy cause."

"Well, thanks, Dane," Bev said, climbing back up onto the cart. "Have a good one."

"I'll see you in town a bit later!" He hopped the fence back into his property. "Planning on spending a few hours looking at all the sights."

"See you then!"

Bev met up with the miller, Sonny Gray, who loaded her up with another half-dozen ten-pound bags of flour. It was, perhaps, overkill, but Bev wasn't taking any more chances. It had been hard enough to get away today, and as the festival went on, things would get much busier at the inn.

She didn't stay long to chitchat, heading right back toward town as the sun rose higher in the sky. It was probably about nine o'clock, and her dough should've risen enough that she could continue the bread-making process.

"'Lo, Bev."

Trent Scrawl stood at the corner of his lot, a rake in hand as he watched Bev and Sin roll down the road. Bev put on a bright smile for him, even though he was scowling at her. She couldn't blame him. She'd caught him draining the Pigsend creek to water his pumpkin entries, and for a moment, accused him of being the cause of the sinkholes in town. They hadn't been on friendly terms since, though Bev was ready to let bygones be bygones.

"Morning, Trent. Excited to see what you present at the festival in a couple days," Bev said. She peered behind him to glance at the pumpkins. "My, my. They've gotten even bigger since the last time I saw them."

"Haven't been doing anything underhanded, if that's what you're thinking," he said, twisting his hands around his rake. "And I seem to remember you promising you wouldn't—"

"And I won't tell a soul," she said, putting her hand to her heart. "Besides that, once those soldiers left town and all the, uh…well, everything returned to normal, all the other farmers in town seem to have their crops back to full strength. So I don't think we have to worry about you getting an unfair advantage."

"Except *they* have an unfair advantage with that whatever you called it, magical river, running under their land." He scowled. "I've half a mind to tell the judges about *that*."

Bev couldn't argue with him. She'd read in an agricultural book that farmers were encouraged to find magical rivers as they chose a plot to grow their gardens. But that book was banned, magic was a taboo subject, and Hendry's warning about the queen's representative was still fresh in Bev's mind.

"I think between the two of you, enough tomfoolery has gone on for the year, eh?" Bev said. "So maybe let things lie for the moment? Next year, feel free to complain as much as you want."

"Harrumph."

Bev didn't care to talk more with him, so she waved and goaded Sin forward, eager to get back to the inn as quickly as possible.

Back home, Bev put Sin back in her stall and unloaded all the bags into the kitchen. It was a little warmer inside than Bev would've liked, but when she checked the risen dough, it was a fine height and smelled great.

"Ah, here you are." Petula Banks stepped out into the kitchen with her usual look of annoyance. "I do hope those muffins on the counter weren't an indication of your baking skills. They left a lot to be desired."

Bev's brows rose in surprise. "The ones out on the counter? They were made by the baker across the street."

"Well, good thing *he's* not entering the contest." She snorted. "Needs far more work in my eyes. And I've tasted my fair share of muffins from across this great country. My palate is exquisite. The queen herself has said so."

"I see," Bev said, suddenly regretting her decision to enter at all. Something told her nothing would be good enough for Petula's *exquisite* palate. "What can I do for you this morning, Ms. Banks? I'm about to get my hands dirty with some more rosemary bread, but if you need something, I can tend to it later."

"Just to see if the rumors were true," she said.

"You will be submitting something to the contest?"

Bev wore a tight smile. "If I can get it done in time."

"Surprised you didn't make an extra loaf last night."

Wim's voice was loud in her mind, reminding her to be polite, even in the face of rudeness. "You know, next time I may do that."

Petula looked around the kitchen, almost as if she were looking for something. "I've heard great things about this bread, you know. For such a small town, it's quite well-regarded. As part of the competition, there will be a requirement to list all ingredients used."

"Flour, barm from my own beer, water, salt, and rosemary from my garden," Bev said. "And a little bit of love, of course."

"I see." Petula walked the length of the room, lifting the lids on Bev's stores of other spices and the ingredients on her shelf. "You've got quite the collection here."

"Should be harvesting the garden for the winter soon," Bev said. "Usually after the festival's over. But the rosemary is year-round, so I use it as I need it."

Petula picked up one of the jars and sniffed it before putting it back.

"Is there something you're looking for?" Bev asked, after a moment. "I'd be happy to show you where it is."

The other woman made a sound of annoyance as she turned on her heel to face Bev. "Well, it's about time for the festival to begin. Lots to look at today." She nodded at the dough still untouched on Bev's table. "Hopefully, I'll be seeing you before five this evening. That's the deadline for submission, you know. Must be fair to all the competitors. It's in the handbook."

"Of course, of course," Bev said. "Well, if that'll be all, I'll get back to baking."

Petula eyed her as if annoyed to be dismissed and not the one doing the dismissing, but turned and left Bev in the kitchen.

Chapter Four

Petula's odd behavior, coupled with the frenzy of trying to get everything done and a few more interruptions from some of the other guests, meant Bev was *very* behind schedule when she finally got her loaves of bread in the oven.

But it was done, and when she pulled them from the oven, they were beautiful and perfect— perhaps even a smidgen more golden brown than yesterday's loaf. But it was after four, and the loaf had to cool before it could be sliced and eaten. It would be cutting it close, but it might be all right.

The rest of dinner was in the oven, several large pork shanks in a bed of root vegetables and broth.

Bev hung up her apron and, as much as she hated to do it, she actually locked both doors to and from the kitchen, in case there *was* some kind of rosemary-bread thief. She could survive without submitting to the competition, but she absolutely could *not* go one night without serving bread to her customers.

Wrapping her contest entry in several tea towels, she pulled off her apron and checked her reflection in the front hall mirror before leaving the inn behind. Ida and Vellora were talking near their front door, though it seemed a...decidedly *unhappy* conversation. So she ducked her head and rushed by them, hoping they wouldn't consider her eavesdropping on a discussion between wives.

Even before she reached the front of town, it was packed. The clock atop the town hall was visible from all angles, so Bev kept an eye as she was stopped by local townsfolk and out-of-towners alike to chat about the comings and goings of the festival.

"Bev! Is that what I think it is?" Gilda Climber, the blacksmith's apprentice, came walking over with a smile on her face.

"Indeed. Gotta head to the contest now." Bev sidestepped her with an apologetic smile and kept walking.

"Good luck!" Gilda called. "I know you'll win."

"Bev? Entering the bread-making contest?" Gore Dewey, Gilda's boss, turned to grin at her. "About time we brought a ribbon home to Pigsend!"

"We'll see what happens," Bev said, walking up the steps to the town hall and letting herself inside. Once the noise of the festival died down, Bev took a deep breath and walked to the front where a row of tables was set up.

Petula Banks glanced at her pocket watch and sniffed—was that unhappily?—as Bev made her way to the front.

Bev put on her best smile as she placed her bread onto the table and signed her name next to it.

"Do make this one of the last ones you slice into," Bev said with a smile as Petula walked by. "It's not been an hour since I pulled it from the oven."

"Your lack of time management isn't our concern," Petula said with a haughty look.

"Oh, come now, Petula," Claude said with that charming, youthful grin. "I'm sure we can cut Bev a little slack—"

"We absolutely can *not*." Petula turned to him. "And you, sir, have a lot to learn about festival competitions if you want to become an official arbiter." She lifted her small nose in the air as she stormed away.

Bev let out a low whistle and finished adding all her information to the placard. "Thanks for the assist, Claude. Good luck working with… Well, good luck with all that."

He made a knowing face. "Say no more."

Technically, the judging was anonymous, but Bev failed to see how that would work considering the varieties of bread on the table. There were a few perfect-looking rye loaves, three sourdoughs as golden as Bev's, plus a couple filled with various dried fruits. Bev counted at least twenty breads and wondered how her still-cooling loaf would measure up.

"Mr. Bonding and I will now depart to the sheriff's office," Petula announced. "Ms. Witzel will plate up each bread and bring it to us in the judging room. Once we've made our decision, we will return."

Ida stepped forward with a knife and a stack of plates in hand. Perhaps hearing Bev, she started at the opposite end of the table and sliced pieces off each loaf, marking them with a number and giving that number to the baker. Down the line she went, and Bev waved her hand in front of her loaf to expedite the cooling process.

"First competition?" asked the man to her right. He was perhaps a head taller than she was, with clay-colored skin and short black hair. He had an air of superiority about him, but his was the prettiest sourdough on the table, to Bev's eyes.

"Yeah, didn't plan on entering," Bev said. "Had something of a mishap this morning with the loaf I was going to enter."

"It happens. Once you've been baking longer, you'll be better able to manage your time."

Bev straightened and gave him a look. It took everything in her not to ask him if he knew who she was, and she immediately hated the feeling. *This* was why she didn't do contests like this. It brought out the worst in people.

But it was polite to introduce herself, so she offered a kind smile to her fellow contestant.

"I'm Bev, by the way," she said. "I own the Weary Dragon Inn here in Pigsend. I don't think I've seen you around before."

If he recognized the inn, he didn't show it. "Stanton Bucko. From Middleburg."

"Well, welcome to Pigsend," Bev said, forcing herself to be nice. "Glad to have you in town."

"It's a fair distance to come here, of course," he said with a weary sigh. "Takes me away from the business world. But I do love to bake, and I find I'd like to add to my collection of ribbons this year. I've got ten of them, you know. Longest streak in Pigsend history."

"My word," Bev said. "That's certainly something to be proud of."

"Indeed." He glanced down at her loaf. "You know, bread needs to rest before it's cut into. The temperature—"

"Yes, as I said, I was scrambling a bit," Bev said, needing to stop him before she was ruder than she wanted to be. "I had a whole loaf that walked away this morning. Strangest thing." She tapped her fingers on the table as Ida made her way closer. "I wasn't even going to enter, but Mayor Hendry asked if I would try to bring a ribbon home for Pigsend."

"I see. Isn't that a bit...biased?" Stanton quirked a brow as if he knew the answer to his question.

"I don't see how it is," Bev replied. "Mayor Hendry isn't included in the decision-making process. And I believe we're in good hands with Petula and Claude. They both seem to be excellent at their jobs."

"It's a shame Alice had to step down," he said with a sigh. "Must've been a nasty cold to keep her from coming here. She and I go way back."

Talk about biased. Bev kicked herself mentally. She took a deep breath and tried to find Wim McKee's old, gravelly voice to keep her mind on the right track.

"Well, good luck to you," Bev said. "Not that you need it. That's a pretty loaf if I ever saw one."

"To you as well. If you make it through, hopefully your next loaf won't...uh...*walk off*."

Ida stepped in front of Stanton with a plate and her knife ready. "You'll be number seventeen, Mr. Bucko. Let me slice into this—"

"Actually, I brought my own knife," Stanton said. "Can't be too careful these days. And *that* knife would make a mess of my beautiful crumb."

He brandished a serrated knife he took from his belt and carefully moved it through the bread, cleaving off a single piece in the middle. He placed the slice gently on Ida's plate and dusted away any additional crumbs that came with it.

"There." He smiled. "Is that satisfactory?"

"Sure," Ida said with a look that was nothing if not forced politeness. "Thanks."

She placed the plate and several others on a larger tray near Rustin's office before returning to Bev. "You're going to be number four. Didn't think I'd see you here. You're late."

"I'll tell you about it later," Bev said. "I didn't bring a fancy knife, and I don't care where you slice from."

Ida choked on a snort as she sliced two pieces off the bread, taking the section without the heel and moved on to the next person.

"Do you always bring your own knife?" Bev asked.

"Well, as you know, the knife makes the slice," he said. "And what I mean is—"

"Yes, different blades do different things to the bread," Bev said.

"And I can't trust a judge would have the

correct kind of blade to best showcase my abilities. Not when so much is on the line."

"Mm."

Ida had finished gathering the slices and carried them inside Rustin's office, four at a time. Bev glanced down the line of contestants to see if anyone else was making small talk or milling about, but most of them looked nervously at the judging room, some breaking pieces off their loaves to chew on absentmindedly.

"How long does this usually take?" Bev asked.

"Do you have somewhere to be?" Stanton chuckled.

"Yes, actually. The inn is…" She couldn't see the clock, but based on the shadows, it was getting late. "Well, I'll have to serve dinner soon."

"I doubt it." He puffed out his chest. "Have you been to the festival before? There's food everywhere. I practically have to roll myself back to Middleburg every night. I doubt anyone will want to come to… What did you call it? The Wonky Dreary Inn?"

"Weary Dragon Inn." If he'd been in town as much as he said, he'd definitely have heard about it. Something told Bev he was being willfully obtuse. But she did her best to ignore it. "I had twenty to feed last night, including the eight staying with me at the inn." Again, she glanced at the shadows on the wall. The pork and vegetables would be fine—

the longer they cooked, the more tender they'd be. The bread was already made and cooling. But she actually had to *be* there to serve it. If dinner was late, she'd have a room full of angry guests. And that wasn't worth any blue ribbon.

Ida re-emerged from Hendry's office and plucked four more plates at random from the table then returned inside. Four plates, twenty contestants, five trips. Bev crossed her arms over her chest, debating if she should leave. They wouldn't disqualify her if she wasn't here to hear the results, presumably?

"Stanton, good to see you." Another contestant had finally broken away from behind the main table and walked down. She was very pretty, with smooth black hair as she held out her hand, a guardedlyfriendly smile on her face. "Your bread looks impeccable, as always."

"Aiming for my eleventh best in show," he said. "I do hope you're ready to take the next honorable mention, Felicia."

The woman's eyes flashed warningly. "You never know. I might have a few tricks up my sleeve this year. Been tweaking my rye recipe to get the most out of the flavor. And with all new judges, perhaps a fresh perspective will change some things around here."

"Well, if not," he chuckled, "there's always the

pie-making contest. But then again, you always seem to come up short there."

"Oh, are you entering a pie as well?" Bev asked, hoping to keep them from coming to blows over the loaves. "That's amazing. You must be some baker."

Felicia turned to Bev, eyeing her. "And you are?"

"Bev. Owner of the Weary Dragon Inn."

She wouldn't have thought it possible, but Felicia's eyes grew even darker. "Oh, *you're* the one who cancelled my reservation."

Her name clicked in Bev's mind, and she nodded slowly. "You're Lazlo's cousin. I do want to apologize again for the mix-up. I'd be happy to offer you a free night next year."

"No need, I'm sure. It's been difficult staying with my cousin but not impossible." She glanced at Bev's entry. "It appears your loaf should've cooked longer. You know—"

"I know," Bev said, her patience wearing thin. "I'm aware. I've been baking bread for five years. Unfortunately, it couldn't be helped today."

"Bev has *lots* to do back at her inn," Stanton said. "Perhaps it's best if you left. You seem like you've a lot on your plate, and I doubt..." He smiled, but it wasn't warm. "Well, *if* there's news to share with you, I'm sure your friend over there will be able to tell you."

"If, indeed," Felicia replied. "I can't imagine

they'd let a half-baked bread through to the next round."

"Well, stranger things have happened," Bev said, glancing at the ceiling. "But you're probably right. I do have so much to be getting on with, and Ida will give me any updates." She plucked the rest of her rosemary bread from the table, annoyed it was still so warm. "Will I be required to give more of this, or can I take it with me? Always nice to have more on hand for the dinner guests."

"No, your entry's been submitted." Stanton picked up his half of the sourdough and handed it to her. "But feel free to take some of mine as well. I'm sure a nice sourdough would go well with whatever…dish you're planning to serve tonight." He glanced at her bread, as if judging her *other* cooking from this one example. "I insist."

"And my rye," Felicia said. "Please."

"Great. The more the merrier."

Bev didn't have time to take a breath as the front room was already filling with hungry people, drawn by the scents from the kitchen. She gave them all a quick hello, promised she'd be getting things going in a minute, and ducked into the kitchen. Blessedly, the meat and vegetables inside the oven were perfect, and her other loaves were exactly where they were supposed to be. At least *one*

S. Usher Evans

thing had gone right.

She plated everything and brought it out in stages. As expected, the guests were ravenous, eager to fill their bellies with Bev's cooking. It was a nice salve after meeting Stanton and Felicia to see so many out-of-town folks appreciate the hard work that went into the upkeep of the place.

"Oh, are you trying something new?" Earl Dollman asked as he came to the bread bowl. "What is that? Rye? And a sourdough?"

"Gifts from the bread-making competition," Bev said, a little annoyed when he plucked a slice of rye from the bowl along with her rosemary bread. "I threw my hat in the ring today, but I'm pretty sure I didn't get past the first round."

"That's…" His eyes crossed as he took a bite of Stanton's sourdough. "Good green… That is the most delectable thing I've ever had in my entire life. How is it so… It's *amazing*… And…" He walked away, too entranced with his newfound love for sourdough to continue the conversation with Bev.

She waited for him to go for the rosemary bread, but he came back for seconds and thirds of the sourdough, leaving his piece of rosemary bread untouched.

She shook it off. Ida'd be by soon to tell her she hadn't made the cut, and she could put this whole competition business behind her.

The room was busy, and everyone seemed happy, so Bev took her leave to begin kitchen clean-up and preparations for tomorrow. In the kitchen, her gaze snapped to her window where she realized she'd forgotten to grab another sprig of rosemary from the garden to dry.

"Bev, old girl, you're losing it," she said. It would be a little less dry than she wanted it, snipping it now and using it in the morning, but what could she do?

She walked out into the dark, cool night and headed over to her garden.

Then she stopped short.

Her garden had been completely uprooted. All the plants—including her beloved rosemary—were gone.

CHAPTER FIVE

Bev stared at the garden for at least five minutes, stunned. Then, with legs that seemed to work on their own, she walked to the stable shed and found her trusty lighted mushroom stick. It was exactly what it sounded like: a long tree branch covered in mushrooms that glowed in the starlight. She used it to illuminate the garden, her heart sinking into her stomach as the light showed in clearer detail what she already knew.

It was all gone.

She knelt before the raised box, plunging the glowing stick into the ground above her so she could use both hands. The earth was freshly overturned, crumbling through her fingers. The only thing that remained was the herbs' lingering scent.

Her fingers found purchase on something hard, and she started, pulling the small amulet piece from the ground. She stared at it, recalling when it had first come to light after the sinkhole debacle. She'd assumed it was the thing the soldiers had been in town to find, and a voice deep inside had told her to *put it back and keep it hidden*. So, she'd reburied it in her garden. In hindsight, perhaps not the smartest idea.

And yet...here it was. The garden was uprooted. The amulet barely covered. And whomever had done this hadn't taken it.

"Bev?"

Bev quickly shoved the piece into her pocket as the back door opened, and Ida walked out. The butcher scanned the yard until she found the glowing stick, then, as her eyes adjusted to the night and the destruction was clearer, her hands came to her mouth.

"Oh, Bev. My goodness." Ida rushed over and knelt beside her. "Your beautiful garden. Who would do such a thing?"

"I haven't a clue," Bev said with a faint shrug, even as the amulet weighed heavily in her pocket. "But...it's all gone."

"Sweetie." Ida covered Bev's hand. "Well, I

don't know if this is good news or not, but I was coming to let you know you'd made it through to the next round."

"Oh?" Bev couldn't find it within her to be excited. "I don't think I'll be able to compete. I don't have any rosemary left." She gestured to the empty garden. "Was coming out here to cut some more for tomorrow's batch, and I found it like this."

"We should find Rustin," Ida said with a nod. "This isn't usual. Something foul is afoot."

"Ida, don't jump to conclusions," Bev said. Though it didn't seem too out of the realm of possibility. Bev's loaf had walked away the night before, and now her garden was gone. She'd thought her so-called friendly competition was perhaps a bit on the pompous side but harmless enough. But what lengths would they be willing to go to in order to secure that prized blue ribbon?

"Someone's destroyed your property, Bev," Ida said, rising. "If that doesn't warrant a visit from our local law enforcement, I don't know what does."

Bev tugged her hand to keep her from standing. "This might be a reason to avoid it." With a breath, she pulled the amulet piece from her back pocket.

"What…is that?" Ida asked, tilting her head.

"I'm not sure. I found it last month after the sinkhole debacle," Bev said. "Something told me it was… Well, I think it might've been what Karolina was searching for."

"Why didn't you say anything?" Ida asked.

"Don't think I'm off my rocker," Bev said with a chuckle, "but I think it was…mine. From before, you know? I don't know how or what it might be, or why I decided to bury it here."

Ida stared at her. "You said you don't remember who you were."

"And I don't," Bev said. "But when I found this thing, there was a feeling deep in my gut that told me to keep it buried." She snorted and glanced at the destroyed garden. "Should've picked a different spot."

"Okay, say this thing is…well, what they were looking for," Ida said. "Why would they destroy the garden then leave it behind?"

"I don't know," Bev said.

"I think…" Ida chewed her lip. "Bev, I don't think this is what they were after. It has to be a coincidence, you know? Besides that, who in town is searching for an amulet?"

"Petula?" Bev offered. "Her soldiers?"

"Don't turn into my wife." Ida rolled her eyes. "These soldiers are different. They're nice. Petula, on the other hand… I don't see her ever getting her hands dirty like this. No, it had to be someone trying to sabotage you for the competition. Please, let me find Rustin."

"Fine." Bev held up her hand in surrender. "Just...don't mention this thing to anyone, okay? Not until we know for sure."

"I wouldn't dream of it." She finally got to her feet. "I mean...this magic stuff is ridiculous, you know?"

Bev quirked a brow, but said nothing. Ida was well-known in town for having strength that far surpassed what was possible for a woman of her slight build. But it wasn't until she'd put her hand on an iron machine that she finally reached the limits of her strength, confirming the theory that it came from some kind of magic. However, Ida had shut down any conversation about such things. It seemed she was content to bury her head in the sand and ignore the reason she could lift an entire cow carcass by herself.

"Anyway," Ida said to the awkward silence, "let me find Rustin."

She dashed out of the yard, leaving Bev by herself. Bev stared at the amulet in her hand. What should she do with it? She could, of course, give it to Sheriff Rustin or even Mayor Hendry. Both had promised Karolina if they came across anything magical, they'd let them know promptly. But that same feeling of needing to *protect* this thing came to the forefront, and as Ida practically dragged Rustin back into the yard, Bev found herself hiding the piece back in her pocket.

Rustin had clearly been enjoying some of the festival fare, as he had turkey drippings on his shirt and sugar on his fingers. But his whole face fell as Bev showed him the damage to her garden.

"Well, Bev, this is a shame," he said with a shake of his head. "Probably a wild animal, you know?"

"You think? With all the activity going on in town?" Ida said, eyeing him. "Bev entered the bread-making competition. Maybe someone's trying to sabotage her."

Rustin rubbed his chin. "That seems like a stretch."

"Does it? Stanton Bucko was staring at her bread like it was an affront to his existence," Ida said. "I wouldn't put it past him to pull something like this. Or Felicia Dinwight. She was pretty miffed at Bev for canceling her hotel reservation."

"Now, Ida, we can't start accusing people of stuff," Rustin said with his hands up. "Let me see what I can find out. There are a lot of new people in town this week, so maybe somebody knows something. In the meantime, you two quit thinking about conspiracy theories and get some rest, okay?"

Bev smiled. "No need for that here. I'm out of the competition anyway. I'd like an answer as to who was digging up my garden, that's all."

Ida watched her warily. "No, you're not."

"What?" Bev chuckled. "Ida, I don't have any rosemary. Can't make rosemary bread without—"

"Wait here." Ida spun on her heel and disappeared from the yard, leaving Bev and Rustin alone.

Rustin put his hands in his pockets and whistled. "Have you had a chance to get out into the thick of things yet?"

"No, can't say I have," Bev said. "How are those soldiers in town treating you? Better than Karolina and her group?"

"Oh, for sure," Rustin said with a wide grin. "Me and Ridge Holt go way back, you know. Couldn't believe my eyes when I saw him rolling into town with Ms. Banks."

"Strange the queen is so interested in festivals," Bev said. "Seems like a detail she could perhaps leave to the local folks, eh?"

"The queen likes order, so I hear. Things must be just so."

"Must be why she picked Petula to lead her charge," Bev said with a chuckle. "Well, I'm glad you've had a chance to catch up with your friend, Rustin. They seem like a nice bunch."

"They are!" He chuckled. "And uh…if you don't mind, I was in the middle of eating dinner with the lot of them. Would you mind if I—?"

"Go on," Bev said. "I'll be sure to tell Ida you're

hard at work finding the culprit."

Rustin was gone by the time Ida came back into the yard, and she looked put out that Bev had let him leave. "Am I the only one who wants to see the guilty party come to justice?"

"You know Rustin isn't the one who's going to help us," Bev said with a chuckle. "Besides that, he's convinced it was a wild animal."

Ida huffed. "So what? You're saying *we* should investigate the contestants one-by-one and see who might be guilty of sabotaging you?"

Bev's eyes nearly bulged out of her head. "Ida Witzel, have you lost your mind?"

"No." She put her hands on her hips. "No, something is *funny* about all this. I've been on the Harvest Festival committee for three years now, and while the competition is always fierce, I've never seen this much tension. And just...Stanton and Felicia were staring at you like you were a piece of meat to be devoured."

Bev frowned. "Ida, I really don't think they're capable of—"

"Bev, I know you want to think the best of people. It's what I love about you, along with that rugged optimism," Ida said. "But... But I have to tell you that I think someone's out to get you. And if we want to bring the prized blue ribbon in bread-making to Pigsend for the first time in ten years, we need you to win."

"Just one problem with that," Bev said, gesturing to the garden. "No rosemary to bake with, remember?"

"Well, that's what I went to get." Ida pulled something wrapped in butcher's paper and twine from her back pocket.

Immediately, the scent of rosemary hit Bev's nose. She carefully unwrapped the paper to reveal five sprigs.

"Where did you…?" Bev asked.

"I may or may not pop by once a week to cut a few stems off," Ida said, lowering her gaze as if embarrassed to admit to her crime. "Vellora likes a bit of rosemary in her nighttime tea, and I figured it was such a big plant, you wouldn't mind." She paused, glancing at Bev. "You…don't, right?"

"Of course not," Bev said, turning the stems over in her hand. "Ida, this is…"

"Don't tell anyone I gave it to you," she said. "Just keep it secret until it's time to bake that final loaf."

Bev could've argued it was all pointless, she was going to withdraw from the competition because it was too much of a hassle, but holding the last remnants of the precious rosemary plant she'd tended to for almost five years, she nodded.

"I will." She looked at Ida and smiled. "Thank you."

With the amulet and sprigs in her pocket, Bev moved quickly through the main hall to the second floor, waving off questions from Bardoff and Earl and promising she'd be right down. She opened the door to her tidy bedroom. It was sparsely decorated, with a twin bed pushed under the window, a wash basin with a cloth, and a small dresser for her things. She walked to the dresser and opened the top drawer, revealing her freshly laundered tunics and shirts. She pushed them aside, laying the amulet amongst the linen and wondering if even *that* would be safe.

But her attention was more focused on the five sprigs of rosemary. It would be enough for one more batch of loaves, and for that she was grateful.

Part of what had made her rosemary so good was *this* specific plant. Other rosemary grown elsewhere in the city didn't have the same punch— and Bev had tried it. She wasn't sure how long ago Ida had cut these branches off her plant, but maybe...maybe there was some life left in them.

Leaving the rosemary in her room, she dashed downstairs once more—again ignoring Bardoff and Earl—and headed to the yard. In a pile near her gardening equipment were some ceramic pots she used to transplant herbs she wanted to keep through the winter. She plucked one off the ground, grabbed her trowel, and headed over to her displaced garden.

She filled the pot with her garden soil then went to her pump and wet the soil considerably. Then, determined, she walked back into the inn and up to her room.

In the dim light, she inspected each sprig gently, looking for signs of life. The one that seemed the spriest, she cleared of leaves about halfway up the stalk then stuck into the moist soil. She placed the pot on her windowsill and sighed, staring at it.

"Well, little guy, I don't know if you'll make it," Bev said. "But this is the best I've got for ya."

As for the other sprigs, she wrapped the butcher twine around the top of their stems and hung them above the pot, so they'd dry in the sun. The final round of the bread-making competition wouldn't be for a few days, plenty of time for the rosemary to dry out. So that…that would be fine.

She put her head in her hands, the scent of the earth strong. It was grounding (she snorted at her own joke) but at the same time, helped soothe some of the sadness at the state of her garden. She had a sprig that would hopefully propagate, and she could replant it in the spring. The rest of her garden she could start from seed, as she had before. It wasn't irreversible.

"There you go, Bev." She removed her hands. "Keep your head on straight."

Activity echoed from downstairs, and as much as Bev wanted to crawl into bed, she did have things to tend to. So she washed her hands in the basin and made sure she looked presentable. Then she held her chin high and walked downstairs, a smile on her face.

But for the first time in memory, she actually locked her bedroom door.

CHAPTER SIX

The next morning, Bev once again locked her door, especially when she caught sight of her garden out her bedroom window. It looked even more horrific in the early light, but Bev was determined to put it behind her. Today was a new day, and there was too much to be done to worry about things she couldn't change.

Instead of his usual muffins, Allen had opted for some sweet pastries glazed with sugary icing and different fruit fillings, and they certainly put Bev in a fine mood as she sank her teeth into the raspberry. She promised herself she'd only eat one, though the lemon curd was tempting, and forced herself back into the kitchen to begin her day's work.

Although she didn't have any rosemary, she did have everything else to make the bread, so she grabbed the jar of leftover dough from the day before, barm, flour, and the salt well, and set to her daily task. As she measured the ingredients, she let her mind drift toward Ida and her conspiracies.

Truth be told, if someone had wanted to sabotage Bev's baking, they could've taken her starter and barm and that would've been much more devastating.

She rubbed her forehead with the back of her hand, as she gathered and put it away to proof. The more she thought about it, the more she agreed with Rustin's assessment of a wild animal.

Especially because they left the amulet behind.

"Now, Bev, we're going to forget we saw that thing, remember?" she muttered.

In fact, once this festival was over and the town cleared out, she'd be finding a *more permanent* spot for the darn thing. Perhaps she'd chuck it into the dark forest on the north end of town and never have to think of it again. Whatever purpose she'd had for hiding it before she'd lost her memory didn't seem worth all the trouble of having it so close to the Weary Dragon Inn.

With the bread proofing, she cleaned up her mess and hung her apron on the pin by the door, walking out to the front room to greet her guests for the day.

Ira Bower was already working his way through a pastry. He was something of a regular, having made his reservation for the upcoming year upon checking out of the previous one, and Bev always delighted in seeing him walk through the door.

"Good morning, Ira," she said as she sat on her stool. "Pastries are good this morning, eh?"

"I'd swear it was Fernley herself baking over there," he said, wiping the icing from his lips. "Her boy's finally got the hang of things?"

"You could say that," Bev said, pushing the basket away from her slightly instead of giving into her temptation. "How'd you sleep?"

"Like a lamb, as usual. Say, what are those new knitted blankets made of? I'd like to get my hands on some to crochet with."

Bev smiled. "I can't recall the name of the beast, but they live underground. The knitter himself is submitting to the contest in a few days, I think."

"Oh…" Ira's face fell. "Suppose it's another year without a blue ribbon for me, then. I don't know if I can compete with that craftsmanship."

For all the years Ira had been competing, the sweet man had never once won as much an honorable mention. "Don't say that. I thought for sure my bread wasn't going to make the cut, but it somehow pulled through to the final round."

He smiled. "Yes, but the rosemary bread is delectable. I couldn't help but snag myself a piece before I went to bed last night."

"Say, Ira," Bev said slowly, "you didn't hear anything last night, did you? In the garden?"

"No, why?"

"Well, darnedest thing." She forced a half-smile. "My garden was dug up last night. Or sometime yesterday, can't really be sure. But everything's either been eaten or thrown somewhere. Not even a rosemary sprig left."

"Your garden?" He put his hands over his mouth. "Well, isn't that the... Who in the world would do such a thing?"

"Haven't a clue. Sheriff Rustin is on the case, but you know..." Bev chuckled as she leaned on the counter. "Not sure he's going to be able to devote all his attention to it, considering he's in charge of festival security."

"Well, I do hope you find the culprit and bring them to justice." He plucked the lemon curd Bev had been eyeing off the top of the basket. "Absolutely horrific. Destroying a good innkeeper's garden. Whatever are you going to do about..." His eyes widened. "Oh, what about the bread-making contest? You won't be able to submit if you don't have rosemary."

Bev almost told him she had a couple sprigs upstairs, but Ida's warning was too fresh in her mind. She did trust the old man, but who knew who he'd tell once he left here. "I'm sure I'll find some somewhere. But tonight's bread will have to be the regular kind, unfortunately. Hope that won't be a problem."

"Of course not." He patted her hand. "I'm off to the festival. Have a good one. I hope…" He shook his head as he took a big bite of the pastry. "Goodness. I can't even believe…"

Bev waved him off. "Have a good one, Ira. Enjoy the festival."

Bev asked the other guests the same question, not really expecting them to be much help, but hoping the knowledge that the rosemary was gone would soften the blow for dinner tonight.

Petula was one of the last to make her appearance, and Bev couldn't help but glance at her fingernails to see if there was any dirt under them. But they were pristine and perfect.

"Ugh, is this what we have for breakfast?" She sniffed the basket. "When I return to Queen's Capital, it won't be a moment too soon."

"Sorry to hear your visit isn't going well," Bev said with a forced smile.

Petula seemed to notice her fakeness. "You know, I was surprised to find your name attached to that bread yesterday. I would've thought, based on the temperature when you brought it inside the tent, it would've been too mushy, not cooked. And yet it was perfectly done all the way through." She lifted a brow. "Are you sure there's no tomfoolery afoot in your baking?"

"Tomfoolery?" Bev chuckled. "Like what?"

"You know the use of magic is strictly prohibited in festival competition. Not to mention it's prohibited *everywhere* unless officially sanctioned by the queen." She adjusted her shirt. "And if I were to find any kind of illegal magic use, I'd have to report it to the queen's service as quickly as possible."

"I'm sure you'll find no such magic in my inn," Bev said with a small shrug. "Just got lucky, I guess."

"Hm. Well, I hope your *luck* continues through the end of the festival." She walked to the door. "Have a good day."

Bev watched her go, for the first time, wondering if maybe...maybe the judge might be on to something. Not that Bev was intentionally using magic (she hadn't the foggiest how), but...that amulet had been buried in the garden. What if it had somehow infused magic into the plants grown there?

Was that even possible?

Had Bev been unknowingly serving patrons of the Weary Dragon Inn magic-laced bread all this time? Did that explain why it was so heavenly?

It was enough to make an innkeeper's head spin.

Leaving behind a sign promising she'd return later—not that she expected any of her guests to return for the next few hours—Bev headed back into the kitchen. This time, she made a beeline for the jars of dried herbs on the shelf Petula had been so interested in the other day. She pulled the top off the dried thyme and inhaled deeply. Nothing about it *seemed* out of the ordinary...but was that because Bev was so used to the scent of magical herbs?

Or am I going mad?

It was nearly ten, and she needed to pay a visit to the butchers anyway. So with a question on her mind, she headed across the street.

"How long do you remember the rosemary bread at the inn being delicious?" Bev asked Vellora as she walked inside.

"Excuse me?" Vellora chuckled as she ran her knife through a large piece of beef. "What kind of a question is that?"

"Just trying to make sure I'm not seeing things," Bev said, coming to the counter. "It's always been good, right? I didn't really... I mean, it didn't markedly change when I came along, right?"

"I wouldn't know," Vellora said. "You were already at the inn when I showed up in town, remember?"

Bev made a face. That was true. "Where's Ida? Is she around?"

That was decidedly the *wrong* question to ask as Vellora's face darkened. "I suppose she's busy screwing around with the festival nonsense while I'm here slaving away keeping our business afloat."

Yikes. "Oh. Um. Can I help you with anything?"

"Not unless you can carry these big pieces of meat across the shop." As if proving a point, Vellora grunted as she picked up what was easily a hundred pounds of meat and hung it on a hook. The butcher was a former soldier who'd never lost her strength. But if Ida'd been the one doing the lifting, she probably could've thrown the carcass up there. "Every year, it's the same. She disappears for a whole month. Meanwhile, I've got to keep the town fed all by myself. I tell her to hang up her hat, but she swears no one else will step up to run things." Vellora grunted. "I hear they're talking about moving it to Middleburg. I'd pop open a bottle of wine if they did."

"Oh, but what about all the influx of money we get?" Bev asked. "Mayor Hendry is keen to make sure it stays here."

"Bah, we all make enough," Vellora said. "So what's this question about your bread? Is it because your garden was destroyed?" She glanced around, as if expecting the queen's soldiers to pop out at any minute. "Do you think someone's still searching for that magic object?"

"Yes and no," Bev said. Ida clearly hadn't told her wife about Bev's amulet piece. "Petula Banks said something to me about using magic to bake my bread, and it got me wondering about…well, things. I don't know the first thing about magic, and I don't *think* I have any—"

"Yeah, well, neither does my wife," Vellora said with a low chuckle.

Bev hesitated. "Has she…said anything else about that? It seems like she's content to ignore it."

"She is. Doesn't believe she's got any. But—" the butcher grunted as she picked another carcass off the table and dragged it to the hook, "—you can't tell me a woman her size lifting three times her weight isn't weird."

"I suppose it is a bit strange," Bev said with a kind smile.

"So you think your bread is magical?"

"I don't know. Maybe?" She leaned on the counter. "I suppose I'm more interested in knowing it was my skill that got me to the next level and not some kind of cheat."

"You're a good baker, Bev," Vellora said. "Don't let anyone tell you different."

"Stanton Bucko certainly did," Bev said with a

chuckle. "You know, Ida thinks he's responsible. Or one of the other bread-makers."

"I heard *all* about it last night." Vellora rolled her eyes. "Giant conspiracy to keep your bread from getting the due it's deserved."

"Funny thing is I wasn't really eager to enter in the first place. Hendry convinced me. And all I've been doing since I tossed my hat in is scramble." She let out a breath. "Don't tell a soul, but when I realized I probably couldn't continue, it was such a relief. Then Ida showed up with the rosemary and... well, I feel like I have to now."

Vellora chuckled. "Don't let my wife bully you into anything. If you don't want to participate, don't. And don't let her suck you into her wild theories, either. She's full of 'em. Everything is always some grand conspiracy to her. I think it comes from never leaving this place. Easy to come up with fantasies when you've never experienced the real world."

To an untrained ear, it might've sounded like an insult, but Vellora's eyes had gone distant, the way they did when she thought about the horrors of the war. Bev had never pried—she didn't remember the war and wasn't keen to know more than she did— but Vellora had always given her enough to know those who'd been on the losing side hadn't fared well in the aftermath.

"Even if it *was* sabotage," Bev said, "what is there to be done about it, you know? Dirt can be washed off. It's not as if the culprits are walking around with sprigs of my rosemary on them." She chuckled. "Well, except your wife. And lucky she did. You know, I put one of them in a pot and I'm saying a prayer it takes root. Not that I'm against starting a whole new plant, but..." She smiled. "That little rosemary and I have gone through a lot."

Vellora nodded. "I gotta say, I've gotten spoiled with rosemary in my evening tea. If either of us had a green thumb, we'd grow our own, but we don't, so we leave it to the experts."

"Well, if it does grow, you're welcome to as much as you like," Bev said. "I suppose I'd better be getting back to it."

"What are ya having tonight, Bev?" Vellora smiled. "You never did actually tell me what you're ordering."

Bev could've slapped herself. "Goodness. I'm a bit befuddled, hm? What's looking good tonight, then?"

Vellora eyed the back. "What did we have yesterday? Pork shank?"

"And it was delectable." Bev rubbed her hands together. "Maybe something that doesn't require a whole lot of tending to."

"Let's do another roast, eh? Beef this time. Ten

pounds?"

"Sounds like a plan." Bev smiled. "I'll be back in a few hours to pick it up."

"I'll drop it off. Don't worry," Vellora said. "Or maybe, if my wife wants to show up, she can do it."

Bev didn't like to see the butchers in such disarray, but it wasn't her place to intervene in the marriage. "I'm sorry things are hectic. If I can help in any way, I will."

"Find me some handcuffs so I can keep my wife in the shop," Vellora muttered with a wry smile.

"I'll see what I can do."

CHAPTER SEVEN

Bev stepped out into the sunlight, and perhaps *should* have gone back to the inn to keep an eye on things. But instead, she found herself walking toward the festival, the question about her rosemary bread still unanswered. She did have a few hours to kill, after all, and perhaps she could find someone to give her an objective opinion.

Although the Pigsend town square was as familiar as the back of her hand, there was something about the Harvest Festival that made it seem ten times as big, especially filled with vendor tents and people as it was. Besides the contests, which were always a big draw, people from all over the region came to taste and see and buy. It was hard to pinpoint what to look at first as Bev waded into the throng of people, from the painted wood decor to the smell of fried dough covered in sugar to the demonstrations of the latest farming equipment trends.

A leather goods vendor caught her eye, and she stepped under the awning to inspect his wares. A beautiful pair of boots had drawn her in, but one look at the price immediately turned her off. Bev wasn't above paying good money for good work, but her trusty work boots were in fine condition, and she couldn't see herself getting a second pair because these were pretty (and oh boy, were they).

Near the boots, there were a few bridles hanging on a hook. Sin's was getting a little worn from use, and the price on them was slightly better than what the tanner in town charged, so Bev paid a silver for it and was pleased with her purchase.

Two booths down, Alice Estrich, a local farmer who lived on the west side of town, had set up a booth with all the usual assortment of root vegetables and colorful gourds she sold in the biweekly farmers' market.

Bev grinned as she walked over. "What in the world are you doing here?" Bev asked. "Are all the farmers here today instead of the market?"

She nodded. "Mayor Hendry wanted us to move

the whole thing to town for the festival. I mean, I don't blame her. Ain't nobody going to be headed to our little stands these days. But I'm not selling as much anyway. Would much rather be enjoying the festival than stuck behind this booth." She inhaled deeply. "I keep smelling something fried and sweet, and if I don't find out what it is, I'm going to lose my mind."

"Fried dough stand, down the way," Bev said with a chuckle. "I'd be happy to watch your booth while you go get some."

"Nah. Probably would put me right to sleep if I did." Alice chuckled. "What about you? Inn busy?"

Bev didn't feel like rehashing the drama of the garden, so she nodded. "Seems like Mayor Hendry is trying to impress that queen's person who's in town. She's got me entering the bread-making contest."

"That's what I hear, too." She shrugged. "We have the festival, or we don't have it. Makes no difference to me. People still gotta eat. Not as if I have anything worth entering anyway. Would much rather spend my time growing my wares to make money instead of chasing a blue ribbon."

"And how *is* Herman doing?" Bev asked, knowing exactly who Alice was referring to. Herman was Alice's neighbor and clearly, she'd heard more than her fair share about his nemesis Trent Scrawl.

"Ready for the competition with Trent?"

"It's a blessed month between now and the solstice when he and Trent finally get all their ornery out before it all starts up again. If I didn't have such a robust crop where I was, I'd move just to get away from their bickering."

Bev smiled. Alice's farm was right in the middle of an underground magical river, which provided an additional boost to her green thumb. The farmers hadn't seemed interested in hearing the specifics of why their crops had been failing when said river had been dammed, so Bev didn't mention it.

"Well, how about I grab a couple small gourds from you, to give a bit more flair to the inn?" Bev reached into her pocket and paid one silver. "However many this will buy."

She left with a bag full of multi-colored pumpkins and squashes the size of her fist, happy she'd been able to help out at least one person. It was getting time to head back to the inn, so she turned to go and nearly ran into a solid mass of a person.

"Oh, it's you." Stanton Bucko was holding a large turkey leg and seemed surprised he'd nearly been knocked over.

"Stanton," Bev said, smoothing her shirt. "What are you doing here?"

"What do you mean?" he asked. "I'm in the

competition. Why wouldn't I be here?"

"The final judging isn't for another few days," Bev said. "I thought you'd be back in Middleburg doing... What was it you said you did? Business?"

"Well, I had a later night than anticipated and found a spare room to rent for the evening," he said, shifting a little. "I suppose you found out the news yesterday? So sorry to hear."

Bev blinked, confused. "You mean, about my garden?"

"No, about you not continuing in the competition, of course," Stanton said.

"I'm..." Bev cleared her throat. "I've made it to the next round. Or so I was told."

He blinked at her, and it was clear he'd perhaps heard his own name and stopped listening. "Oh, I must've missed that. Well, congratulations. I'm sure the fact you're the *only* local maker in town had *nothing* to do with your success."

"Have you met Petula?" Bev said with a chuckle. "Everything she does is by the book. Literally, there's a book of rules she follows."

He sniffed. "I see. What was it you said about your garden?"

"Oh, um..." Bev recalled Ida's worried expression and hated how she'd begun to distrust those around her as well. "Nothing. I'm glad you made it through, too. I suppose we'll be seeing each other again in a few days, eh?"

"Indeed." He nodded toward someone on the other side of the aisle. "If you'll excuse me."

He left Bev standing there, and she had the unbearable urge to…find out where he was staying and do some investigation.

Now, that was ridiculous. She wasn't a snoop, that one night in Trent Scrawl's garden aside. But the way he seemed so…convinced she was out of the competition. As if he knew she'd have no way to continue.

"What did he say?"

Bev nearly jumped out of her skin as Ida's voice knocked her from her thoughts. The butcher was grinning madly, as if Bev speaking with Stanton was the most delicious thing she'd seen all day.

"Nothing," Bev said. "Just his usual."

"Oh, come now. I'm sure there's more than that."

"He might've mentioned…" Bev began slowly. "He seemed to think it was impossible I made it to the next round. But that could've been—"

"Because he's sabotaging you!"

"Keep your voice down," Bev said, as a few nearby heads turned to look at them. "Let's not be hasty."

"I heard he grabbed a room in town last night. He never does that. Now why would he need to?"

"He said he had a later night than anticipated," Bev said with a knowing look. "Probably got too deep into the ale."

"Or he spent the night ravaging your garden," Ida said, inching closer.

"And how do you propose we go about accusing him of such a thing?" Bev asked.

"We go find proof." Ida clamped down on Bev's hand. "Because I know where he stayed last night."

~

"This is absolutely bonkers, Ida. I have to get back to the inn and start dinner."

"Ssh."

Ida had all but dragged Bev across town and shoved her into a bush in front of Wilda Murtagh's house. Wilda and Lazlo were siblings, and lived a stone's throw from each other. Wilda's little cottage bore a thatched roof with green walls and a beautiful fall garden out front. Two rocking chairs sat on the front porch, and everything about the place looked to be spiffed up in advance of the festival.

"How can you be sure he's staying here?" Bev asked, peering over the shrub.

"I saw him leaving this morning," Ida said. "His story doesn't add up. Middleburg isn't that far away. Most people who live there come back and forth. So why—"

Bev pinched the bridge of her nose,

remembering what Vellora had said about her wife. "This isn't right, Ida. We can't be snooping around people's private property."

"You didn't seem to care when it was Trent's farm," Ida shot back.

"Because there was a sinkhole in front of my inn," Bev said. "And if I didn't do something, they wouldn't stop. There's no more garden to destroy."

"But there are five sprigs of rosemary," Ida said. "What if they want to break into your room?"

Bev hesitated. Maybe she should consider moving that stupid amulet somewhere *far* away from her herbs. "You're off your rocker, Ida. There's no great conspiracy. It's just—"

"Ssh!" Ida grabbed Bev's shoulder and pulled her down as the sound of conversation echoed from around the back of the house.

"…quaint little town…" Stanton had finished his turkey leg, though the remnants were still visible on his shirt. He was walking with someone Bev didn't recognize, along with…

"Is that Petula?" Ida whispered. "So much for being on the up and up."

"Don't jump to conclusions," Bev said, but it did look rather fishy.

It was hard to hear their conversation through the rustling leaves.

"…the size is a problem. The inn, of course, is

something of a dealbreaker. How are you supposed to host a festival if you only have room to house six people? And while Her Majesty can appreciate the entrepreneurship of opening homes to host, it seems Middleburg would be much better suited for the festival in this region."

"Yes, as I was saying, we have three inns with space to accommodate sixty, at least," the unknown woman said. "As mayor—"

"Whoa." Ida clamped onto Bev's arm, and she winced—it would probably leave a bruise. "The *mayor* of Middleburg's in town?"

"Wonder if Hendry knows," Bev said.

Petula smiled warmly at the two Middleburg residents—the nicest she'd looked since her arrival. "Well, I do appreciate the chat, but I must be getting back to the competition hall. I'm looking forward to the first round of the pie-making contest."

"There are several from Middleburg," the mayor said with a knowing smile. "I believe a sweet potato and two apples—"

"Oh, don't tell me any more," Petula said, holding up her hands. "I take my job very seriously. Anonymity is essential to keeping the competition equal. There will be no special treatment for anyone."

"Not even that insufferable innkeeper?" Stanton

asked.

Bev scowled. She'd said perhaps three words to the man.

"I haven't a clue how she managed to get through to the next round," he continued, looking toward his mayor. "Makes me feel like maybe Mayor Hendry had a hand in things."

"As surprising as it is, her bread was perfectly executed," Petula said. "Perhaps she knows something we don't about the timing of pulling bread from the oven." She pursed her lips, and Bev could practically see the accusation of magic on the tip of her tongue. "But we'll see how the final round goes."

"Indeed." Stanton huffed. "It may be hard to recreate that *perfect* execution a second time."

Ida whacked Bev in the shoulder so hard she almost cried out in pain.

The trio split, with Stanton and the Middleburg mayor headed away from the festival, and Petula headed toward it.

Ida and Bev waited a few minutes before Ida turned to Bev with a knowing look on her face. "Well? What was that about me being 'off my rocker?' Clearly, Middleburg's conspiring to steal the festival from us."

"So we should tell Hendry, and she'll handle it." Bev gestured toward the house. "This isn't the time for us to be— Where are you going?"

"Wilda's in the pie-making contest," Ida said over her shoulder. "She won't be back for an hour. Plenty of time for us to snoop."

⁓

Every instinct Bev had told her to go back to the inn, but she followed Ida into Wilda's kitchen anyway. It was homey, with a wood-burning stove topped with a dinged-up kettle. A wooden table held salt and pepper shakers and a crocheted doily, and several mismatched teacups hung on hooks beneath a shelf bearing tea from the local shop. The floor had been swept clean, and there was a nice, multicolored rug made of fabric scraps that Bev wiped her feet on.

Ida, however, ignored the quaint kitchen and marched right through to the living room. Then, deciding that wasn't good enough, she headed up the back stairwell to the second floor. Bev let out a whimper, torn between following her friend to talk some sense into her and turning around and saving her own skin.

"Hurry up! I found his room!"

Bev let out a breath and climbed the stairs.

"Unexpected night, my foot," Ida said, walking over to Stanton's sizable traveling trunk sitting open under the window. "He's packed as if he was planning to stay for a while. The whole festival."

"He doesn't owe us an explanation about his traveling habits," Bev said lightly, wincing as Ida dug into his clothes. "Ida, we have to go. This is absolutely wrong."

"Ah-hah!" Ida popped upright, holding a pair of boots covered in dried dirt. "Look at this! Proof!"

"Ida." Bev sighed, putting her hands on her hips. "Maybe they got filthy while he was traveling here."

"Bev." Ida brought the boots to her nose. "They smell like herbs."

"So what? He ripped up my garden and stomped on them?"

Bev took the boots and inhaled deeply. There was…something fragrant about them, but she didn't immediately smell any of her herbs. Her gaze darted down to his open trunk, and she reached in to pull out a tin. Inside was a dark paste, probably for rubbing into leather goods like the boots. And the same fragrant smell that lingered on the shoes.

"See?" She showed it to Ida. "Totally explainable. He may be insufferable, but—"

"Beverage Wench." Ida giggled. "That has to be the meanest thing I've ever heard you say about someone."

"Well, I have it in me every so often," Bev said. "Look, we need to get out of here before Wilda or Stanton come back. I understand you want to find someone and bring them to justice, but in this case, maybe it *was* a wild animal. Maybe a bad stroke of luck. Either way, I doubt we'll find the culprit." She put her hands on Ida's shoulders. "Why don't we let this go, hm? We've got rosemary. I'll replant the garden in the spring. There's no need for all this fuss."

"Um, Bev." Ida was in the trunk again. "What do you think this is?"

She pulled out a small wooden sprig. Rosemary.

Bev hated how smug she looked.

CHAPTER EIGHT

Bev trailed behind Ida, who was intent on showing the evidence to Mayor Hendry before any more time passed. She seemed oblivious to Bev's presence, muttering to herself about conspiracy theories and how people wouldn't believe her. Bev was sure she was counting her own wife in that number, and she hoped, perhaps, this little event wouldn't put another rift in their relationship.

They wove through the festival, Ida flat-out ignoring the calls from friends, and Bev offering an apologetic smile and half an explanation. Ida flung open the doors of the town hall, where the pie-making contest was starting.

Petula made a noise of surprise. "Ms. Witzel! You're not scheduled to help out with this competition. What—"

"Where's Mayor Hendry?" Ida asked, raising the sprig of rosemary. "I have—"

Bev quickly grabbed her hand and pulled it back down. "We need to chat with her real quick. Is she around?"

"I'm here." The beautiful mayor appeared in the doorway of her office. "Please, continue with the competition, Ms. Banks. I'm sure everything is just fine."

Without another word, Bev and Ida walked into the mayor's office, and she swiftly shut the door behind them. "Now what in the world is the meaning of this? Don't tell me it's a problem with the queen's soldiers."

She was looking at both of them, but Bev knew the barb was directed at her. "This isn't my show, Hendry. I'm here for moral support," Bev said, holding up her hands.

Ida made a noise. "But it's *your* garden that got destroyed."

"Wait, *what?*" Hendry rose to her feet. "Bev, your garden was… What happened?"

"No clue. Last night, I went out to clip some rosemary for the bread, and I found it completely destroyed. All the plants were gone."

"And *I* think someone is sabotaging her," Ida said. "Stanton Bucko, for one."

"I dislike that blowhard as much as the next person, but you can't accuse people without proof," Hendry said.

"I have proof," Ida said. "We saw him talking with Petula Banks and the mayor of Middleburg—"

Hendry's dark eyes narrowed immediately. "Miranda Twinsly."

"They were talking with Petula about the competition," Ida said. "Seemed like Stanton didn't think Bev got through on her own merit *and* didn't think she could recreate the loaf she made, which made me super suspicious, so we broke into Wilda Murtagh's house—"

Hendry let out a loud groan. "You can't walk into people's houses looking for things. And even if you *did* find something, it's not anything I can use because you got it illegally—"

"But I found a rosemary sprig!" Ida said, holding up the plant. "It's from Bev's garden."

"Can you prove where you found it—and that it's *definitely* Bev's?"

Bev watched the back and forth with a sense of déjà vu. During the sinkhole debacle, Bev had come to Hendry with the same frenzied sort of desperation to be believed, and Hendry had responded with the same measured and, in hindsight, *sane* response.

Ida, however, looked how Bev had felt, which was unheard and unhealed. "Seriously, Jo? You aren't going to do anything about this? Don't you want to keep the festival in town?" Ida asked.

"Of course I do, but this isn't anything I can fix with what you've given me. Yes, I'm sure there's something funny going on with Miranda Twinsly being in town. Yes, it's suspicious that Bev's garden was destroyed—"

"And I suppose I should mention that the competition loaf I'd baked went missing the night before," Bev added lightly. "But it could've walked away."

"Right," Ida said with a dubious look.

"All of this should be looked at, absolutely," Hendry said. "Have you spoken to Rustin? He should be the one in charge of investigating."

"He thought it was a wild animal," Ida said. "I don't think he's the right man for the job."

"Be that as it may, this *is* his job, so I'm going to have to ask both of you to cool it." She folded her hands on top of her desk. "We're already on thin ice as it is with Petula, and if we get a bad report, she *will* cancel the Harvest Festival and move it elsewhere. So let's pretend we're all one big happy family and try to keep any more mishaps from—"

A loud yell echoed from the room beyond, and

the three women shared a look before scrambling out. Lining the wall of the meeting space, there'd been no fewer than forty pies on two different tables —except now, one of those tables had been knocked over. All the pies on top were in multicolored, gooey piles on the ground.

The wail had come from Wilda Murtagh, who was on her knees in front of what appeared to be an apple pie that was now a gloriously delicious mess.

"My beautiful pie!"

"What in the world happened?" Hendry cried, running into the fray. "Petula? Claude?"

"I have no idea!" Claude gasped. "We were speaking with the contestants, informing them of the rules. All of a sudden, we hear this big crash and…" He gestured to the floor. "What a mess."

"What a catastrophe!" Etheldra Daws wailed as she stood over a chocolate mousse pie. "All that work…"

"Tell me you at least got a slice of it," Ida said softly. "Right?"

Claude shook his head. "Not yet. We were about to start that process."

Bev sighed, shaking her head. "I'm sure it was an accident."

"The good news," Petula's voice rang out true and loud, "is that we have a protocol for this sort of thing. It wouldn't be fair to use this pie to judge. So we'll reschedule the entire contest for tomorrow morning. And make *triple*," she glared at Hendry, "*sure* that the tables are set up correctly so this sort of thing doesn't happen again."

"Of course," Hendry said weakly. "Of course, absolutely. Here, let's get all this cleaned up."

Even though she needed to get back to the inn, Bev stuck around to help sweep up the sticky, sugary mess on the floor. It was tempting to grab a spoon and try each and every one, from the bright yellow lemon curd to the warm chocolate pie to a cranberry-apple tart that smelled as good as it looked. But Bev swept the remnants into the dustpan and dumped it in a trashcan out back, shaking her head at the waste.

The rest of the pie-makers had vacated quickly, those with pies left to share carrying them like precious commodities. Petula had recommended each baker remake theirs to be at "peak taste and quality," but it remained to be seen how many folks would be able to accomplish such a feat. Many of the bakers had used the last of their summer fruit to make their pies and perhaps had enough for the final round of judging, but not for this extra round.

Hendry listened to the griping, especially those from out of town who insisted they wouldn't be returning next year, and caught Bev's eye. There was something unspoken there, something Bev couldn't quite understand, but she got the gist. Whatever was going on, *someone* needed to figure it out before the whole festival ended up cancelled.

Her bread was in danger of being over-proofed by the time Bev finally ran back into her kitchen. It was going to be a disappointment regardless, thanks to the lack of rosemary, but she still had a minimum standard she liked to adhere to. Vellora had delivered the ten pounds of beef, too, and guilt weighed heavily on Bev's shoulders. Instead of talking her wife off a ledge, Bev had jumped off with her.

Now, of course, Bev had a very fatty piece of meat that needed slow cooking under low heat for many hours...and she didn't have that last bit anymore. But she wasn't without her tricks. She sliced the meat into smaller pieces, laying them flat on the bottom of her cast iron pot. Then she poured a mixture of vinegar, salt, and spices over the top until all the meat was submerged. The vinegar would help break down the meat so it was more tender, and the salt would help as well. It wouldn't be the best dish she'd ever made, but it would do for the evening.

At the end of the day, she was happy to be back in the silence of her kitchen, with the sounds of the fire and her knife slicing through potatoes. Instead of roasting them, she peeled and tossed them in a large pot with water and salt. For some extra flavor, she tossed a few pieces of parsnip into the pot, and sliced the top off a head of garlic and put it in the oven to roast. When the potatoes were cooked through, she drained them and added them to a large bowl with a bit of the cooking liquid. She plucked the garlic from the oven and squeezed the roasted cloves out into the steaming potatoes. She added a few scoops of salted butter and mixed it all together, tasting and adding additional salt as needed. Within minutes, it was a fragrant, buttery white cloud.

It was, unfortunately, the only part of dinner that came out well. The beef, while edible, was still on the tough side when Bev plated it up and the bread was... Well, the bread was never going to be good, but it was all right.

As she ran her knife through the loaves, she again wondered about Petula's accusation, that she'd been using *magic*. The accusation took on more weight as she took a bite and found it... underwhelming.

"Nothing to be done about it now, Bev, ol' girl." People were hungry and dinner was in need of serving.

She carried out the plate of beef first to loud applause, and it was hard not to cringe knowing she wasn't serving them her best. But within moments of putting the platter down, the table was swarmed. Bev ducked into the kitchen to grab the mashed potatoes, and like with the beef, it, too, was well-received. But when she came out with the basket of bread, the response was underwhelming.

"What is this?" Etheldra said, holding up the loaf. "Where's the rosemary?"

"Sad news," Bev said. "Someone ransacked my garden and destroyed all my plants. There was no more rosemary for my bread tonight."

"*What*?" Etheldra's cry was so loud it silenced the entire room.

Bev's cheeks warmed considerably, and she cleared her throat. "It's fine. I'm sure I can grow new plants in the spring. But we'll be without the rosemary bread for at least the next few months."

"That is absolutely *not* fine," Etheldra huffed. "What scoundrel is responsible for this egregious miscarriage of justice?"

"Well, we're not quite sure," Bev said, not wanting to bring up Ida's conspiracy theories. "But there's nothing to be done about it now. The plants are gone, and we're going to have to carry on."

"What a *shame*." Stanton Bucko appeared seemingly out of nowhere, which was a feat considering his size and ego. "I hear the rosemary was the best part of your bread."

"Stanton," Bev said with a tight smile. "Whatever are you doing here?"

"The word on the street is that you've got the best dinner in town," he said. "So I had to come and see for myself what all the fuss is about."

Bev huffed. Of *course* the night Stanton showed up at the Weary Dragon was the night her dinner wouldn't be up to her usual standards.

"It's not my best," she said, knowing she sounded ridiculous. "Unfortunately, I got swept up in the chaos at the pie-making contest. Can you believe it? A whole table was knocked over. Just a shame and a half."

"You know, these sorts of things wouldn't happen in Middleburg," he said. "I can tell Pigsend's resources are stretched thin. You don't even have a standing committee, just a haphazard group of folks like that butcher."

"I think that Pigsend is a lovely town," Claude said, coming up beside him. "I can certainly see why Aunt Alice loved coming here year after year."

Stanton sniffed. "Well, I do hope that you're planning on something spectacular for the final round of the competition, Bev. If this loaf is any indication, you certainly got lucky the other day." He cracked a smile. "And I believe the official rules state that the bread submitted must be *exactly* the same recipe. Hard to do that if you don't have any rosemary."

"I'm sure I can rustle some up from somewhere," Bev said, keeping her tone even. "I'm not the only person in town with an herb garden."

The words hung in the air, and Bev waited for Stanton to challenge them or say something that would give away the fact that he knew she and Ida had been snooping in his rented room. But he smiled and grabbed another piece of the bread.

"I'll be headed back to Middleburg in the morning," he said. "Unfortunately, I can't spend the whole week on vacation here in this...lovely town. But rest assured, I'll be back for the final day of competition."

"Well, have a safe journey," Bev said, though she was dying to know if he was taking any of her herbs back with him. Perhaps he hadn't noticed his piece was missing.

He turned and went to sit down with the same lady Bev had seen him with before—the mayor of Middleburg. They had a quick conversation and he caught Bev's stare before she turned back to Claude and forced herself to forget them. She wasn't on the case—there wasn't a case to be had, even. Time to get back to being the hostess she was trained to be.

"I'm glad you're having a good visit, Claude. You should come back when things aren't quite so crazy," Bev said. "Pigsend is lovely in the winter.

Everything slows down a bit, and people spend more time by the fire. The farmers get a break from their fields and get more social. The Witzels even throw a huge winter solstice party." She smiled. "I make a delicious wassail that might be as delectable as the rosemary bread..." She sighed. "Which it doesn't look like I'll be making any time soon."

"Absolutely ghastly," he said. "I saw it as I was coming in this afternoon. Just from a pure plant-lover perspective, what in the world was the point of that?"

"Honestly, Claude, it's probably a wild animal," Bev said, growing weary of talking about it. "How was the first day of the festival? Minus the pie catastrophe."

"Brilliant, of course. I can't believe I never came here before. It's been the most thrilling day of meeting people and tasting things." He ducked a smile. "Don't tell Petula, but I might have snuck a few bites of some of the competition pies before the competitors left. It was too good to pass up!"

Bev promised she wouldn't tell a soul, and Claude returned to the table to continue his meal. In their usual spot, Earl Dollman, Etheldra, and Max Sterling were eating and conversing together, and Bev thought about asking them the question she'd posed to Vellora earlier in the day.

But as she began cleaning up the plates and

counting the pieces of bread left in the bowl, the answer was clear—there *was* something about that rosemary that made the bread taste better. And as sad as it was to admit, perhaps it was for the best that Bev's unknowing use of it had come to an end, at least for now.

After the last bowl was gathered, Bev retreated into the kitchen. She was bone-tired and would've much rather left all the cleaning for the next morning, but that was asking for trouble. So with a sigh, she plucked her wash basin from near the back door and carried it out to the yard.

She was pumping water into the basin when she heard a noise. Stopping, she turned to scan the darkness and waited to hear if it would sound again.

She shrugged then went back to her business.

But the noise came again, and this time Bev swiped her glowing stick from near the back door and shone it over the yard.

"Hello?"

She wasn't sure what she'd been expecting, but the small, floppy-eared dog with yellowish fur standing on top of her compost pile was certainly not it.

Chapter Nine

Bev's first instinct was to shoo it off, but there was something about the shape of his face—almost too small for his body, with droopy ears and big, golden eyes almost the same color as his coat—that melted her heart. She knelt and held out her open palm for him to sniff. He came closer, hesitantly flicking his tongue to lick her, and his tail wagged as she patted him on the head.

"Where did you come from, little guy?" Bev asked, scratching his ears.

He walked closer, moving her hand down his back until it reached his hindquarters. He grunted and shook his rear with happiness as she scratched harder.

"You're a funny little dog, aren't you? What's your name?"

He didn't have a collar, and Bev hadn't ever seen him around before, so she assumed he must've come with one of the festivalgoers. When he turned around to smile at her with his tongue hanging out, he had something wooden stuck in his jowls.

"Is this thyme?" Bev gasped as she pulled it out.

The dog reared up on its hind legs and snatched the wooden stem, dashing away with it like a thief stealing a gem.

"Wait!" Bev cried, hopping to her feet. "Come back!"

He moved fast for such a small animal, and Bev had to jog behind him to keep up. He had a silly sort of run, almost as if his front half was going left and his back half was going right, and yet Bev was huffing and puffing as she chased him out of the village and into the dark night. Thankfully, the moon was full and bright overhead, so she could at least see where she was going.

He ran into a thicket—not the dark forest, but still thick and brambly. With his size, he was easily able to navigate the roots and thorns, but Bev had a tougher go of it. Her shirt sleeve ripped on a large branch, and something whacked against her cheek, but she pushed through, wishing she had her kitchen knife or something else to slice through the brambles.

"Here, little fella," Bev called, letting out a whistle. "Where did you…"

She finally came into a clearing where the dog was nestled on top of a big pile of…herbs. The scent hit her nose immediately—thyme, basil, parsley, marjoram… Bev's entire uprooted garden had been turned into a dog bed for this creature.

He lifted his head and wagged his tail as she approached. Gently, she ran her hands through the pile of plants, all the way down to their dirt-covered roots. As she'd thought, someone had ripped them out, roots and all.

"Did you do this?" Bev asked.

The dog, predictably, nuzzled her hand in search of a pet.

"I don't see any teeth marks," Bev said, inspecting one of the thyme plants closely. "And you'd have to be a much bigger sort of creature to have carried all this here in one go, eh? So maybe someone else just left it here, and you liked the way it smelled?"

As if proving her point, the dog rolled onto its back and started smushing his rear into the plants.

"Wait! Wait!" Bev cried, moving the dog off the plants. "Don't kill them. I need them for my garden."

The dog allowed itself to be moved and flopped back into a sitting position to watch as she separated the plants from one another, picking the most salvageable and laying them out flat next to her. The dog might not have been the one to take the plants here, but he hadn't done them any favors by sleeping on them. Either way, she had enough now that she could dry and store her herbs for the winter, and perhaps save a few for propagation.

"You didn't see a rosemary bush anywhere around here, did you?" Bev said, looking up and gazing around the small thicket.

The dog tilted his head.

"No, that would be way too lucky," Bev said, climbing to her feet as she gathered the plants she intended to take home. "Thanks, I guess. Sorry I'm taking your bed, but these belong to me anyway. I'm sure you've got an owner who's looking for you, huh?"

He plopped his rear on the ground and looked up at her, dead serious.

"Why am I talking to a dog?" Bev muttered, turning around and leaving the thicket the way she'd come.

The dog had followed her back, but she didn't really mind. She closed the kitchen door behind her, leaving the animal outside where he belonged, as she inspected her plants in better lighting.

A loud whine echoed from the back door, along with a loud *scratch*.

"Are you..." Bev put down the marjoram plant and marched to the back door, swinging it open. Before she could say a word, the dog dashed inside between her legs. "Oh, no. You don't get to come inside. Go on. Outside. Out. Go!"

She grabbed her broom and began sweeping at the dog, but he dodged her blows, almost as if he thought it was a game. Finally, she ditched the broom and grabbed him by the midsection. He was a *lot* heavier than his size would suggest.

"You've got a home, I assume. So go there," she said, opening the kitchen door and tossing the dog on the ground. "You can't stay here."

She closed the door swiftly but didn't get two steps before the whining and scratching began again. Bev pinched the bridge of her nose and vowed to ignore it, returning to her plants spread out on the kitchen table. It was hard to think with the loud wailing, but she pressed on...

...until she remembered she had an inn full of guests upstairs who probably *wouldn't* appreciate the sound.

"Good*ness*," she grumbled, walking back to the door.

As before, the little creature dashed inside, a

joyful look on his face.

"Fine," Bev said. "You want something to eat? I'll feed you. Then you have to go home. You can't stay here."

She hadn't yet thrown her potato peels into the compost pile out back, so she put the bowl on the ground and the dog went to town, scarfing them as if he hadn't had a proper meal in weeks. Bev felt bad for him, so she found a bowl and filled it with water.

"Was that all? Were you hungry?" She tutted. "Sorry. Eat up. Then get on your way."

With the dog happily chomping away, Bev returned to her plants and came up with a game plan. Much like the rosemary upstairs, she would try to replant the garden in pots over winter and hope they took. The rest, she'd dry and pulverize.

She turned to get a set of pots from the back garden when she realized the dog was staring at her. He had *devoured* every single potato skin—and based on the look on his face, it wanted more.

"I have nothing else for you," Bev said with a shrug.

He followed her as she walked out into the yard to search for her planters. She was acutely aware of his presence as she filled more pots with soil and brought them back inside. She prepared the herb branches and stuck one in each pot, adding enough water to soak them through.

"What?"

The dog was staring at her expectantly again.

"I have no more food for you. And that was a *lot* of potato skins," Bev said. "Surely, you're full, right? If you eat any more, you'll turn into a potato."

He tilted his head, waiting.

She let out a breath. "I'm talking to a dog. This is ridiculous."

She put the newly planted herbs on her windowsill—she hoped no one would be interested in messing those up—then cleaned the dirt off the kitchen table and carried the remaining pots and trowel back outside.

When she came back into the kitchen, she let out a yell of surprise.

"*Get down!*"

The dog had somehow *jumped up* onto the kitchen table and had his little pinkish-brown nose in the herbs. He scooted off the table at her yelling, jumping to the floor and running to the corner to cower.

"Okay, dog, you *have* to go," Bev said. "Because I'm not putting up with this anymore." She walked to the door and opened it. "Out you go."

He tilted his head.

"Out."

He blinked.

"*Out*, you little—"

"Bev, who in the world are you talking to?" Mayor Hendry walked through the front door of the kitchen, looking her usual perfectly put together self. Her dark eyes scanned the room until they landed on the creature in the corner. "When did you get a dog?"

"He's not *mine*," Bev said with a huff. "He was skulking around my compost heap earlier. I chased him to a thicket about five minutes from here where I found the remains of my garden."

"The rosemary, too?" Hendry asked, hopefully.

"No, unfortunately," Bev said with a sigh. "But everything else, thankfully. This little guy had been sleeping on it, I guess. Now he's followed me home, and I can't get rid of him." She looked up at the mayor. "You don't want to take him, do you?"

"Oh, heavens no. I'm a cat person." She held up her hands in surrender. "And besides that, we have much to talk about. Namely, the pie contest."

"I'm only a bread-maker," Bev said, walking to the plants on the counter and making sure the stupid dog hadn't destroyed them. "And that's in debate today."

"I'm talking about who overturned the table," Hendry said. "I don't think it was an accident."

Bev stopped. "And? Why are you telling me?"

"Well, you know. You're…well-versed in this sort of thing. Finding the truth."

She straightened. "Didn't you *just* tell Ida and myself to cool it?"

"I told *Ida* to cool it. She's on the festival committee. How would it look if she was out accusing our contestants of sabotage?" Hendry raised a brow. "You, on the other hand, are a contestant. A contestant who's been wronged. And it's absolutely understandable that you'd want to find out who might be responsible for wronging you."

"That's not—" Bev turned quickly at the sound of something falling. That damn dog was stretched as far as his little body would go, trying to get his long tongue into the jar of butter on the table. She crossed the kitchen to move it out of his reach and hissed at him. "Why do you think it wasn't an accident?"

"Because it's too... Nobody in that room would *accidentally* tip over a table of pies, Bev." Hendry put her hands on her hips. "There has to be a reason behind it."

"And what's your theory?" Bev said. "Middleburg?"

She nodded. "Maybe Mayor Twinsly put one of her contestants up to it. Just to show that we aren't capable of hosting a festival."

"Haven't we hosted this festival for the past—"

"It doesn't matter. We're no longer under the

old rules," Hendry said. "But if you and Ida are already looking into Stanton Bucko, maybe you can find out where the mayor's staying. I've tried, but she tells me she's returning to Middleburg." Hendry's gaze darkened. "Lying liar of a woman."

"And what, exactly, do you want me to find?" Bev said, keeping a wary eye on the dog as he yet again attempted to reach the butter. "Stanton Bucko said he was going back home."

"Something to prove that the Middleburg delegation is trying to ruin the festival."

Bev sighed. "And when am I supposed to do that? I've got an inn to run, bread to bake for the competition *you* want me to be in—"

"You'll figure it out. I believe in you." Hendry turned to walk toward the door. "And a word of advice? Ditch the dog. Nobody wants to eat out of a kitchen where a dog's been licking the food."

"Are you—" Bev spun around. That *darn* dog was nose-deep in her butter jar. "Get out! Scat!"

The dog yelped and ran away toward another corner, licking its jaw and nose aggressively. Bev looked inside her butter jar and found a knife to scoop out a good half-cup of butter to get to a part that hadn't been slobbered on.

"Now I have to go buy more," Bev said, looking at the jar. "Why can't you keep your snout out of stuff it doesn't belong in, huh?"

The dog was too busy sniffing and licking every morsel of butter off the floor to listen.

She sighed, putting her hands on the table. She should probably hang the rest of her plants to dry, but she was tired, the hour was late, and all she wanted was to go to sleep. So she gathered the herbs and put them high on a shelf, knowing that even if this stupid dog somehow managed to sneak his way inside, he wouldn't be able to climb all the way up there. Then she turned to the creature, who was still searching the cracks in the floor for any last remaining butter.

She knelt in front of him and held out her hand. He happily ran over, searching her for more good things to eat, and when she had none, he went back to sniffing the floor.

"You certainly are food-motivated," Bev said, patting him on the butt. "But unfortunately, Hendry is right. Can't have a dog in my kitchen. It's unsanitary."

She once more took him around the midsection and carried him out toward the yard. This time, however, she kept walking until she reached the thicket where she'd found his little bed and set him down in front of it.

"I'm sure whoever's life you make miserable is missing you right now," Bev said, scratching his velvety ears.

The dog leaned into her hand, closing his eyes and groaning happily.

"But my life is already complicated enough, and I don't need to be spending my time keeping you out of my various food stores, you hear?" She kept scratching, now holding him up as he relaxed fully into her hand. "You're obviously well-fed, based on your size. You don't need my food. So go on home."

She stopped scratching him and stood. The dog stared at her, tilting his head to one side as he did, and Bev stared back.

"Well. Goodbye."

She turned to walk toward the inn, but the sound of four feet following stopped her after three steps. The dog stared up at her with that expectant, determined little look he had, and she tilted her head back.

"What do you want from me?" Bev asked. "You can't stay in my kitchen. I'd be out of everything by morning."

He stared at her.

"I don't have anywhere else for you to stay. It's not as if I'm going to let you sleep in my room."

The dog wagged his tail.

CHAPTER TEN

The next morning, Bev woke up with a furry ball awkwardly positioned between her ankles. It had taken one round of loud wailing and scratching from the dog for Bev to give in. Bev didn't trust him in her kitchen, so she'd brought him upstairs and given him a nice blanket to sleep on. When the little bugger had woken up and crawled into bed with her, she hadn't a clue, but it was *the first and last time*.

He growled as she got up, and she glared at him. "Absolutely not."

The growling ceased, and his tail wagged.

"First things first, we've got to figure out who

you belong to," Bev said as she washed her face. "And get them to take you back."

She inspected the rosemary hanging in the window and the one planted in the small pot. The hanging rosemary was drying well and would be more than ready when Bev needed it. But the potted plant didn't show any signs of life—and it looked a little wilted. Bev sprinkled a little more water onto the soil from her wash basin and patted the ceramic bowl.

"Grow, little guy, grow," she whispered. "You're all I have left."

She turned and realized the dog was still curled on the bed, his golden eyes following her as she wandered around the room.

"Get off the bed." She pointed to the floor. "Don't even know how you got up there in the first place. Go on. Get."

The dog made a loud yawning noise as he rose to stand. He stretched his front paws as far as they'd go, revealing the claws and segments of his toes. His feet were white, almost like he was wearing socks, and there was a patch of white down the front of his chest, as well, that Bev hadn't noticed the night before.

His butt was still high in the air, his tail curling around his back. He opened his mouth to reveal his tongue—pink with some black spots—and let out another yawn. Then he scratched his ear and jumped off the bed, leaving a very obvious circle of dog fur behind.

"Great," Bev said. "Now I have to do laundry. When am I going to have time to do that, hm?"

He plopped his rear on the floor.

"Just don't get too comfortable," Bev said, walking to the door and opening it. "Because today, we're finding your owner."

The dog bounded down the stairs with that same misaligned gait that was almost comical, then headed straight into the kitchen, pushing the door open with his nose.

"Yes, indeed," Bev said, following behind. "Find your owner."

She set to her morning chores, finishing the process of drying the herbs she'd salvaged the day before and checking on the rest of her plants. It was too soon to see a difference for those, but maybe they were a bit livelier than the night before.

Next, she walked outside to feed Sin, and, of course, the dog followed. He stopped two steps beyond her back door and lifted his left leg to relieve himself on her pile of pots.

"Oh, come on," Bev said. "You can't do that there—"

But he was undeterred, leaving a large puddle. When he was done, he walked back to the door, as if expecting to be let back in.

"Not yet," Bev said. "If you're going to hang around, we have to do chores."

She walked into the stables, whistling a good morning to the old mule as she went to retrieve her rake to find Sin some hay. The dog hadn't followed her, and Bev had a small hope that maybe he'd *finally* gone home—until she brought Sin out into the pen to eat and get some fresh air and found the dog chowing down on the scraps in her compost heap.

"You know what?" she said as he ate away. "Eat garbage. What do I care?"

She opened the door to her root cellar and retrieved a few carrots for Sin, while also doing a mental inventory of the rest of her vegetables. Tonight, perhaps she'd roast up the sweet potatoes, maybe with some pork. It wouldn't taste the same without her rosemary, but she could make do.

A loud braying—followed by barking—caught her attention, and Bev rushed outside to find the dog barking at Sin with the hair sticking up on the back of his neck. The mule was chewing on her hay and watching the dog with an *"are you kidding me"* expression on her face.

"Oh, calm down, you stupid mongrel," she said with a shake of her head. "This is Sin. She was here before you. So you'd better be nice."

Sin brayed as if making Bev's point.

The dog stopped barking, but his hackles still stood upright.

"I've got to get to work," Bev said, putting her hand on her head. "You two play nicely."

She walked toward the door, intending to slip inside before the dog could follow her, but he was fast for his size, and dashed between her legs and back inside, sitting in the corner that had fast become his favorite spot. Bev sniffed, accepting she wasn't going to be rid of him in the next few hours, and set to her morning bread-making.

He was actually quite well-behaved, stretching out to lie down in the corner and not making a peep. It was a far cry from the mischief he'd caused the night before, and in some part of her mind, Bev could see how he could be a nice dog to have around. For someone else, of course.

She worked mindlessly, grateful to have a few minutes where the dog wasn't trying to eat something or someone wasn't trying to spin wild conspiracy theories. When it was finished, she found the warmest spot in the kitchen—something of a feat, considering the chill in the air. But it wasn't cold enough to warrant a kitchen fire.

After clearing her mess, she hung her apron by the door and walked out into the front hall. Allen hadn't dropped off his wares yet—it was still early—

so Bev knelt by the hearth to start a fire. But as she grabbed her kindling from the small pile, there was a little golden-furred head sniffing the ashes.

"Get out of there," Bev said, pulling him away from the fire. "It's gonna be—"

He sneezed, sending ashes out in a stream.

"Whatever."

She started the fire, and the dog seemed to have enough self-preservation to keep away, instead immediately sprawling out in front of the fire and falling back asleep. Within seconds, the sound of his soft snoring was audible across the room.

"I mean, as long as you aren't getting into trouble," Bev said.

She propped open the kitchen door to let in some heat and help the dough along. She moved the bowl closer to the heat source, and when she was satisfied, settled onto her stool behind the front desk. It was nearing seven in the morning, so the guests would start walking downstairs any minute now.

The front door opened, and Allen came rushing in with his basket. "A thousand apologies, Bev. Got a bit too ambitious this morning and my meringues didn't set up right. So I had to scramble to make a backup—I hope it's okay."

"Of course it is," Bev said, peering into the basket. Inside were two dozen hard discs made of flour, butter, and milk, still steaming from the oven. "Breakfast biscuits?"

"Yeah, Mom always used to bake them when her pastries wouldn't set, too," Allen said. "She said pair it with some cheese and fried bacon, and nobody'd say a word against you."

"Fernley was always a smart woman," Bev said, noting the other basket of cheese and bacon. "Watch yourself."

Allen frowned and followed her gaze. The dog had awoken and had his paws on the basket, sniffing at the bacon. "What…is this?"

Bev pushed the creature away, but he came right back in search of the bacon. "Damn dog. Found him in my compost pile last night. He'd been sleeping on the remnants of my herb garden—"

"You found it?" Allen asked, lifting his basket higher.

"Not all of it," Bev said. "The rosemary was gone, but the rest of it, yes. No clue how it got there. But anyway…the dog brought me there, and now he won't leave." She paused. "He doesn't look familiar to you, does he?"

"Nope." Allen put the baskets on the counter before kneeling and reaching out to let the dog sniff his hand. "Aw, you're a sweetie, aren't you?"

"He smells food," Bev said dryly.

Allen took a biscuit from the basket and offered

it to the dog, who promptly snatched it from his hand and swallowed it in two bites. "Poor little guy. He must be hungry."

"He ate five pounds of potato skins last night," Bev replied with a look. "And half a cup of butter. I think that's how he is."

"Do you want another one?" Allen said with a laugh as the dog came back with an eager look on his face.

Bev scowled as the baker put together a biscuit sandwich of dried meat and cheese with a dollop of strawberry jam on top and handed it to the dog, who practically inhaled it. Then he stared up at Allen, expecting more as if he hadn't just eaten.

"Well, you aren't kidding," Allen said, patting the back of his head. "He does like to eat, doesn't he?"

"You seem to get along great," Bev said. "Why don't you take him?"

"He seems happy here," Allen said, putting the food out of the dog's reach and scratching his ears. "What's his name, anyway?"

"Not giving him one because he's not staying."

"You're calling him dog?"

"Or 'hey you.'"

"Why don't we call you..." Allen smiled. "Mr. Biscuit. That seems like a perfect name for you. Since you like biscuits so much."

"We could also call him Mr. Potato Skins and Butter—"

"Oh hush, Bev," Allen said with a laugh. "I think the inn could use a little mascot. Kind of helps keep the place feeling homey."

She clicked her tongue. "If that'll be all, Allen."

He laughed. "I'm headed into the festival in a bit to watch the redo of the pie-making contest. I'll ask around and see if anyone's missing a dog—"

"Food fiend."

"—like Mr. Biscuit here." He scratched the dog's ears again. "And in the meantime, you be a good boy for Bev, you hear? If you're looking for delicious food, this is the place to set up shop."

"Don't encourage him," Bev said, climbing onto her stool.

Allen wasn't the only one who was charmed by the golden-eyed little creature. Each guest who came down shared a biscuit with the dog, commenting on how pretty his eyes were or how soft his fur, or how hungry he seemed to be, and that Bev should be sure to fatten him up. Based on his current size, Bev didn't think that was necessary, but nobody seemed to want to listen to her.

The only one who Biscuit didn't take a shine to was Petula, because *of course he didn't*. The moment she appeared, he growled, the hair on the back of his back standing upright.

"What in the world? Whose dog is this?" Petula said, backing up a few steps.

"I'm so sorry," Bev said, grabbing the dog by the scruff of his neck and practically throwing him into the kitchen.

"What's going on?" Claude asked, running down the stairs behind her. "Is that a dog I hear?"

"Yes." Bev plastered a smile onto her face. "I'm so sorry. He showed up last night and I'm trying to find his owner."

"I didn't think this inn was one for animals as well," Petula said with a raised brow.

The darn dog kept barking on the other side of the door, and Bev excused herself. She grabbed the dog by the middle again and tossed him out into the back before returning to her guests. The sound of barking was still audible, but not nearly as loud.

"I promise I'm finding his owner *today*," Bev said, resuming her spot at the front desk. "This isn't the level of quality I expect to provide."

"I should say not," Petula said, eyeing the biscuits, meat, and cheese. "What in the world is this? Some attempt at a bread?"

"They're biscuits," Bev said. "Kind of a local delicacy here. Breakfast biscuits, in this case. You can make a sandwich with the cheese and meat, if you like. Or just add the jam. Whatever you prefer."

She took a bite. "They're dry."

"Well, that's why you add the jam, Petula," Claude said, helping himself and taking a bite. "Magnificent. My compliments to the chef."

"In this case, it's Allen," Bev said. "But I'll pass along the compliments. Good luck today in the redo of the pie contest. Hopefully, everything goes smoothly."

"It had *better*," Petula said, smoothing her shirt. "We've had enough *mishaps* for one festival."

~

With Petula's warning in mind, Bev headed toward the festival to find the dog's owner so there would be no more mishaps. She didn't have to ask the dog to follow her, because he seemed to be permanently by her side. Just when she thought he might've gotten distracted by this or that scent, she'd turn around and find him even with her ankles, tail wagging and mouth open in a smiling pant.

Bev stopped at every vendor booth, but each one was the same—cute dog, not theirs. Bev wouldn't be deterred, though, as the damn thing kept jumping up onto the vendor tables in search of whatever smelled amazing.

"Can you get your dog off my table?" one of them asked, pulling a whole turkey leg away from the dog's long tongue.

"Not my dog," Bev said, pushing him back to the ground. "Is he yours? Or does he look familiar?"

"Can't say that he does."

An hour went by, and Bev was starting to run out of vendors. She glared at the dog, currently munching on a piece of fried dough he'd snatched from a small child. His entire snout was covered in sugar now, and he sneezed as he tried to clear it.

"Well, that's why you shouldn't steal fried dough from babies," Bev chided. "Look, why don't you stay here among all these delicious foods, and I'll go back to the inn and forget you ever wandered into my life, okay?"

He turned, heading back toward the fried turkey legs and Bev hoped against hope that maybe, just *maybe* he would take the hint.

But she didn't make it far before she was accosted by Mayor Hendry, whose dark eyes were wild as she took Bev by the arm.

"Have you found anything on Middleburg yet?"

"No, and I'm not going to," Bev said with a shake of her head. "*You* can investigate. I've got to get back to my inn and get things ready for dinner."

"Bev, I'm begging you," Hendry said. "We can't lose this festival. I—" Her eyes darted down. "I see you still have the dog."

"He seems rather attached to me," Bev said dryly. "Which is a feat, considering all the food here."

"Well, I want you to keep an eye on Twinsly," Hendry said. "She's currently in the pie-making contest, but that's nearly over now. See where she goes after that."

"But I can't—"

"I'm counting on you, Bev!" Hendry floated away, leaving Bev standing in the middle of the road shaking her head.

"I'm not going to follow the mayor of Middleburg," she said.

The dog at her heels sat and stared at her.

"I've got to get back to the inn. The bread will be done proofing soon. And I've got to go to the butcher, too."

More blinking.

Bev growled. "*Fine*. We'll go to the pie-making competition. But only for a bit. Then we really have to…" She stopped. "Why am I explaining myself to a dog?"

He opened his mouth to smile at her.

CHAPTER ELEVEN

With the little dog following her, Bev walked into the town hall, which was fuller than the day before. At the front of the room, only sixteen entrants remained, standing nervously behind their pies, some of them looking like they'd stayed up all night long to get another entry put together. Behind them, Petula's soldiers stood at attention as they kept a wary eye on each participant. The tables themselves had been swapped out for ones that looked heavier and harder to topple over.

The pies had already been cut, and the slices were waiting on another table outside of Rustin's office—just four left, so the judging was almost over.

Ida would surely breathe a sigh of relief once those last four had been tasted and adjudicated.

Bev took a seat in the back and the dog jumped up beside her, curling into a ball and falling asleep. She scanned the room, searching for Mayor Twinsly, but it was hard to pinpoint anyone with their heads facing away from her. She tutted and rose from her perch, wandering up a few rows—the dog, of course, following.

"Oh my *gosh!*" Stella Brewer put her hands to her face and squealed. "Who is *this* beautiful little guy?"

"No clue," Bev said, her focus on finding the mayor in the crowd. "Do you want him?"

"I couldn't," Stella said, picking him up and pulling him into her lap. Beside her, Vicky Hamblin let out a similar sound as she petted him.

"But what a beautiful baby. Oh, you've got the softest ears, don't you? What a beautiful—I mean *handsome* boy you are."

The baby talk continued but Bev tuned it out. At least the dog would stay out of trouble with them. She didn't want to *think* about what might happen if he got too close to the pies.

Finally, Bev spotted the Middleburg mayor up front, wearing a smart tunic and pants. She didn't have Hendry's innate beauty, but she still oozed sophistication, her mauve lips perfectly painted and nary a fire-red hair out of place. She wore a look of amused superiority, as if she expected the whole place to explode into a chaotic mess at any minute.

Bev took an empty seat three rows behind her and waited. Ida took the last of the pies into Rustin's office, and the crowd's murmuring grew. A short time later, Petula and Claude emerged, the latter wiping his mouth with a napkin. "Contest entrants, we've made our decision."

Twinsly sat up straight and smiled, as if expecting to hear all *her* people were the winners.

"Number four?"

Felicia Dinwight stood, a satisfied smirk on her face.

"That was a perfectly executed strawberry rhubarb pie," Petula said with a nod. "You've made it to the next round." She looked at the scroll again. "Number six?"

Five people in total were chosen—two from Pigsend and three from Middleburg, including Felicia.

"This concludes the first round of the pie-making contest," Petula said, sounding very much as if she were reading out of her thick rule book. "Contestants, please clear your entries from the room so we can make way for our jam-making contest this afternoon."

The pie-makers who hadn't made the cut

grumbled as they gathered their wares and walked toward the front door. Some were surrounded by what Bev could only assume were friends and family, who offered words of comfort. Others continued out the door, throwing their pies into the open trash as they left.

"Well, that's a waste of good pie," Bev said with a sigh.

In the front of the room, Twinsly was conversing with the winners from Middleburg. The mayor actually looked disgruntled; had she expected a clean sweep?

The sound of nails on wood made her look down. The dog had found her and climbed up onto the bench next to her. He lifted his nose into the air and sniffed, his ears perking up. Then he jumped, as if headed toward the front of the room to eat the remnants of the pies.

Bev grabbed him before he got too far. "Oh, no you don't. You've caused enough trouble."

She kept him firmly in her lap, even as he squirmed and wriggled to get out. He was hard to keep hold of, twisting this way and that as he scratched at the air to free himself.

"Bev, right?"

Bev stopped, looking up at the voice. Twinsly was staring at her, an amused smile on her face.

"Uh—Yes. I'm Bev. Of the Weary Dragon Inn.

Aren't you Mayor Twinsly?" The dog broke free of Bev's grip and dashed toward the front of the room, disappearing under the table with his nose pressed to the ground. "It's nice to meet you. I saw you in the inn last night."

"Indeed," she said. "Your inn is quite lovely." *For Pigsend.* The unsaid part of her sentence hung in the air.

"I'm fond of it myself," Bev said, keeping a wary eye on the dog sniffing and licking the floor like a creature possessed. "Are you staying in town?"

"No, unfortunately, not many places to stay around here," she said. "I hear you're the only inn. Just *six* rooms."

"That's right," Bev said.

"Forgive me if I don't agree with the assessment that Pigsend is the best place to have a Harvest Festival," she said with a sigh. "Not that your town isn't *lovely*, of course. But so much more could be made of this event if we had a larger infrastructure."

"Mm." The dog was now on his hindquarters, his tongue stretching as long as it could.

"Well, I suppose I'd better go find myself some lunch. We're expecting a good showing from our Middleburg jam-makers," Twinsly said. "Have a good one, Bev."

"And you as..." A loud crash echoed through the space as the dog tipped over the table.

"Scat!" Ida came running into the front of the room. "Whose dog is this?"

"Uh, be right back," Bev said, tipping her head toward the mayor. She rushed up to the front and grabbed the dog by the back of the legs, pulling him away from the table.

"Bev, goodness," Ida said, pushing the table back upright. "Do you know who this mutt belongs to?"

"At the moment? No." Bev used her leg to keep him from reaching the table again. "But if you find out, please let me know, because he won't leave me alone."

"I saw you talking with the mayor," Ida said, her voice dropping. "What was that about?"

"Nothing at all," Bev said with a smile. The dog had become distracted by something else and was trotting toward the trash at the back of the room. "Just being friendly. Good luck with the jams! I have to go."

She rushed down the center of the room after the dog, but he scampered out into the open square. But as Bev turned to follow the mischievous animal, Twinsly's fire-red hair glinted in the sunlight, catching Bev's attention. She was walking away from the festival with Felicia and one of the Middleburg pie-makers. They seemed deep in conversation…almost suspiciously so.

Something furry brushed against her legs. The

dog had returned.

"Well?" Bev sighed. She did still have time before she had to get back to her bread. "I guess we're gonna follow them. Try not to muck this up, will you?"

The mayor's vibrant hair was like a beacon, making it easy to follow her and the other two from a distance. Bev didn't like this feeling—Twinsly hadn't done anything wrong. Being in town wasn't a crime. Hendry was perhaps being driven by some professional jealousy as well as an overzealous desire to maintain the Harvest Festival locally. And though Bev doubted that Sheriff Rustin would arrest her for trespassing, it also wouldn't look great if she was caught snooping around someone's house. She'd been in hot water with the town during the sinkhole fiasco, and she sometimes got the feeling that, although the true culprits were found and expelled from the town, some still held a grudge against Bev.

The Middleburg trio left the main festival route, which was odd if they were looking to find lunch before the next contest, and walked down the mostly residential street. Without the crowd, it was harder to keep out of sight, and there was no good reason for Bev to be walking up this way—

—which left her no choice but to dive into a nearby yard when they stopped to have a conversation in the middle of the street.

She was too far away to hear what they were saying, and she didn't trust that she could get any closer without alerting them to her presence.

Plus, she had a new problem. In her haste to hide herself, she hadn't realized *which* lush front yard she'd ducked into. An ominous cluck echoed behind her, and her heart stopped. Slowly, she turned to stare into the beady little eyes of a chicken with a puff of feathers atop her head. Bev swallowed. This was Rosie Kelooke's yard. She had a large brood of Krooke chickens, a special breed, with a plume of brightly colored feathers that fluttered in the breeze—and they were *mean*. Bev still bore a few scars from the last time she'd tangled with them.

"Nice chicken," she breathed. "I'll be out of your hair in a minute. Just go back home."

Another chicken clucked nearby. Heart pounding, Bev mentally calculated if it would be less disastrous to reveal herself than to be mauled by these demon chickens again—

The little dog appeared beside her, baring his teeth in a low growl. Bev held her breath, hoping he wouldn't start barking because that would *definitely* give her away.

The chicken stared at him, the feathers on its back raising as the dog inched closer. Miraculously, the chicken backed up a step, then another, then fluffed its hind feathers as it walked in the opposite direction.

Bev let out a sigh and patted the dog on the head. "Good boy."

She clammed up quickly as footsteps approached. Twinsly's perfect boots walked by, this time alone. Bev craned her neck to see where they might've gone, but they were nowhere to be found. Once Twinsly was around the corner, she rose and hopped the fence to safety.

"What do you think?" Bev said, looking down at the dog.

He tilted his head up at her.

"You know," Bev said, rubbing the back of her neck, "I guess I should call you by a name, hm? Just until we find your owner. Calling you *dog* isn't working for me anymore."

The dog sniffed loudly.

"Allen might've been onto something. Mr. Biscuit seems like a good name for you," she said, looking up and down the street. "Biscuit for short, of course. Or Mr. B, depending on the context."

He opened his mouth, and his tongue spilled out in something that resembled a wide smile.

"Okay, Biscuit," Bev said, looking ahead, "we've got maybe half an hour before I need to get to the inn. We could—and should—just head back. I think…"

Biscuit seemed to have gotten a whiff of something good because he took off toward the house across the street.

For a small dog, he was *fast*, and Bev could barely keep up with him. Whatever he'd scented, he was locked in, because he didn't slow down at all, even when he wriggled under the closed back gate of...Lazlo Murtagh's house, Wilda's brother. Bev groaned. She didn't want to break into someone's home—again—but she needed to get that darn dog before he destroyed something.

"Wait!" Bev called, opening the gate and running after him. "Hang on. Don't—"

The door hadn't been closed all the way, and with one strong swipe, Biscuit opened it and let himself inside.

"Jeez," Bev said. "Hello? Lazlo? Are you here? My dog got into your house... I mean, it's not my dog, but..."

There was no answer anyway, so Bev stopped talking. She pushed open the back door, expecting to see Biscuit nose-deep in whatever was on the stove or counter, but he wasn't in the kitchen—nor in the small living room.

"Hello?" Bev called. "Not trespassing. Looking for an overly curious mutt."

Something fell hard upstairs, and Bev dashed up

to the second floor. Of the four doors, one was open, with a little sunlight spilling out. She pushed open the door and sighed—Biscuit was inside the open bag of clothes on the ground.

"Are you serious?" she said, pulling the dog off the bag. "You can't just rifle through—" Something hard in his mouth clacked against his teeth as he tried to chew it. "What do you have? Come on, spit it out." She held her hand out, but Biscuit didn't cooperate. "Come on, you little pig, give it to me. Give it. Come on. Give it."

He wouldn't be persuaded, so Bev put him down and pried his jaws open, releasing one small marble-shaped bauble to the ground.

Bev let out a gasp of surprise and swiped it from the floor before the dog could grab it again.

"This is…"

Bev had seen one of these before. They came from a creature called a barus, who was something of a magical wish-granter. He could manifest magic from any creature and give it to a non-magical person in the form of these little baubles. For a price, of course. Allen had been using him to bump up his baking, although he'd found out the hard way that baruses charged higher and higher prices the more times they were visited.

Bev stared at the bag, which Biscuit was no longer interested in as he sniffed the floor, looking for the bauble Bev had in her hand. Inside, she found a jar filled with red berries suspended in syrup and handwritten ingredients for pie crust. She didn't want to jump to conclusions, but she absolutely could see a scenario where someone was using this barus bauble to enhance their baking.

Now, Bev didn't know all the rules in Petula's book, but she was pretty sure *this* was the sort of thing that would get the Middleburg delegation in trouble. If someone was making their pies using this thing, Petula would have a field day…

…and that person would be arrested.

Bev lowered her hand, chewing on the side of her lip. Magic was tightly controlled, even out here, and she had no doubt Petula Banks would order her soldier escorts to put everyone in the house in handcuffs. Was keeping the festival in Pigsend worth it?

Bev didn't know, but winning a blue ribbon probably wasn't reason enough to send someone to jail. She was putting the bauble back inside the bag when the door opened.

"What in the green earth are you doing in my room?" Felicia Dinwight stood in the doorway, holding her strawberry-rhubarb pie, her mouth open in surprise.

"Oh!" Bev spun around and plastered the most innocent look she could on her face. "I'm terribly sorry. My dog got loose, and it seems your pie filling drew him all the way up into your room. I found him nose-deep in it."

Felicia shot a look at Biscuit, who was sniffing around the floor like a dog possessed. "I see."

"I don't think he destroyed anything," Bev said, pointing to where she'd found the bauble. "But I'm terribly sorry. He's a mischief-maker." Bev reached down to pick him up. "Again, I apologize."

"He didn't find…" she began, almost nervously. "Never mind. It's fine. No harm done."

"I'm so sorry, again," Bev said, covering her heart with her hand as she inched toward the door. "Please, come by the Weary Dragon Inn this evening, and I'd be happy to give you a complimentary dinner."

"That's—"

"Bye now!"

CHAPTER TWELVE

Bev busied herself with dinner preparations—a good distraction from her mortification at being caught snooping, and it gave her time to think about that…well, she was quite sure that was a barus bauble. Whether it was the pobyd magic Allen had been seeking to enhance his baking skills or something else entirely, she didn't know.

A low growl echoed beside her as she skinned the sweet potatoes. "You've had enough to eat. I can smell your gas from across the room," Bev said. She nodded toward the corner, where she'd put a blanket on the floor. "Go on. Go lie down."

The dog walked toward his spot and sat on his

bed but didn't stretch out. Bev was used to his constant attention now, but it was better if he watched her from a distance rather than being underfoot.

"Now, where was I?" Bev said, reaching for another potato.

Ah yes, the barus bauble.

If she went to Hendry with what she'd found, the mayor would certainly march to Petula's room with bauble in hand and claim the mayor of Middleburg was behind it all. Which was plausible, of course, but not provable yet.

She paused. Stanton had not only brought his own knife, but also cut his own slice of bread, and handed Ida one from the middle. At the time, Bev had chalked it up to him being particular and wanting to put his absolute best foot forward. But now... What if there was a barus bauble stuffed inside his loaf as well?

"Stop it."

Bev wasn't talking to herself, but to Biscuit, who'd wandered back over to sit by her side and beg for a scrap. He climbed up on his hindquarters and reached his snout toward the sweet potato skin hanging perilously close. Bev rolled her eyes and knocked it to the floor where it was gobbled up in seconds.

"There, you monster," Bev said. "No more,

though. Seriously. I haven't a clue where you put all this food."

And yet...yet he'd gone straight for the bauble. He'd been able to smell it from halfway down the street. Was it a tasty-smelling bit of magic, or was there something else that Bev didn't know about this little dog?

"Knock knock!" Ida walked through Bev's back door with a large hunk of meat on her shoulder. "I... That dog is still here?"

"Unfortunately," Bev said. "He's quite attached to me now for some reason."

"Do you keep feeding him?" Ida asked, as Biscuit trotted up to her, eager to sniff what she'd brought.

"Not willingly." Bev didn't want to tell Ida about her trip into Lazlo's house, though she was sure word would eventually spread around town. "He gets into everything. Spend half my time keeping him from eating my whole kitchen."

Ida gave him a look. "Doesn't look like he could eat that much."

"Looks can be deceiving." Bev reached into her purse and handed Ida a few gold coins. "Thank you for delivering that. How are the contests going?"

"I've got to get back for the jam contest," Ida said. "But I think Vellora was about to hang *me* on a hook if I didn't deliver at least a couple of the meat orders today."

"I know she misses the help," she said, hoping she sounded neutral.

"She doesn't get it," Ida said. "When I was a girl, the Harvest Festival was the *only* thing worth looking forward to. Nothing else happens around here. If we lost it…" She shook her head. "Our little town will shrivel into nothing."

"Yes, but you still have a business to run," Bev said gently.

She made a face. "Anyway. This is my last stop, then I'm headed in to make sure the jams don't end up on the town hall floor again. What a mess, right? Any idea who might have knocked it over?" She leaned on Bev's kitchen table. "Maybe the same person who stole your bread? Lots of mishaps with this festival this year. Can't be coincidental."

"Well, I did find out where someone stashed my garden," Bev said. "Not the rosemary, of course, but the rest of it. Found it in a forest five minutes from here. That dog was using it as a bed." She nodded to the window. "Salvaged what I could and dried out the rest."

"He's good for something, at least."

"Saved me from Rosie's chickens, too," Bev said before she could stop herself.

"What were you doing in Rosie's yard?" Ida tilted her head. "Were you snooping?"

"They escaped," Bev lied. "One was ready to chase me down the street, and Biscuit scared him off."

"Biscuit?" She chuckled. "Oh Bev, this dog is yours. You've given him a name."

"Allen gave him a name," Bev said. "I'm merely using it until I can find his owner."

"Mm." She paused. "Oh, by the way, the knitting contest has been moved to tomorrow afternoon."

"That's nice."

"You were going to get Merv's entry, remember?" Ida said. "And take me with you?"

"Oh. Oh!" Recognition dawned, and Bev could've slapped herself. "Right. I completely forgot about that. Should we head out there in the morning?"

"I have to be back by eleven to help with the quilt-making contest," Ida said, walking toward the door. "See you first thing!"

⁓

Merv had been invited to the festival, but when told about the number of people who'd be in attendance, and that it was outside, he'd immediately declined. Instead, Bev had offered to bring a knitted piece to be entered into the yarn contest, and to that, he'd happily agreed. Thank goodness Ida had reminded her; with all the chaos from the dog and the festival mishaps, it had completely slipped her mind.

Biscuit spent another night sleeping between Bev's legs in the most awkward position possible and did his best to remain underfoot while she took care of her morning preparations. There hadn't been as many complaints about her rosemary-less bread the night before, mostly because she'd rubbed the outside of the bread with several cloves of garlic.

Ida arrived at nine sharp, and the two set off toward Merv's home, with Biscuit trailing behind.

"He is kind of cute, when he's not getting his nose into everything," Ida said.

Bev nodded, holding her tongue about him finding the barus bauble. "But I've got enough to be getting on with, and I don't need to add a dog to the mix."

"You keep saying that, but he's got a bed in your kitchen."

"Whatever."

Merv was a mole man who lived far beneath the village. To reach his humble abode, Bev first had to walk out of town until she found a large hole in the ground. Then it was another twenty or so minutes in the dark tunnel, mostly at a steep decline. Bev had brought her trusty glowing stick to help them see, but it was still very difficult to manage.

"You weren't joking," Ida said, holding onto the

wall for dear life as they climbed down. "This is dangerous."

"Merv doesn't think so."

"He also has long claws if memory serves," she grumbled as Biscuit navigated easily beside her. "They seem to be helpful."

"Almost there."

They reached the bottom, and Bev lifted the glowing stick high above her head as the path smoothed out.

"So this whole world exists under Pigsend?"

"I wouldn't say it's under the village, per se," Bev said. "Maybe to the side of it. But close enough that the earthquakes damaged his home."

Which led to his emergence in the first place. Nobody in town even had a clue he was down there (save Eldred Nest, who'd brought it up at nearly every town meeting). Then one day, he popped out of the ground, demanded Bev do something about the ground shaking, then invited her over for a cup of tea as they worked through what could be causing it.

"Is that it?" Ida asked.

Up ahead, a large, round door blocked their path. It was painted orange with green trim, with two glowing mushrooms on either side and a knitted rug out front.

"Merv?" she called as she knocked. "It's Bev."

There was a noise on the other side, and the door scraped open, revealing a mole larger even than Vellora. Black fur covered him from tip to tail, all except for his bright pink snout where whiskers twitched happily.

"Bev! And you've brought, what is that, a laelaps?"

"No, this is Ida," Bev said. "The butcher."

"No, the other thing. The small thing." He leaned down until he was nose-to-nose with Biscuit. "You're an odd little bugger."

"He's just a dog," Bev said. "A mischievous dog."

"To what do I owe the pleasure?" he said, stepping back. "Come in, come in. Let me put on a kettle."

"We can't stay long," Bev said, brushing her feet on the mat to keep the dirt outside. "But you'd mentioned you wanted to submit something for the Harvest Festival? The judging's happening this afternoon, so I thought I'd pop in to see if you still wanted to."

His whiskers twitched happily. "Well, you know, I don't know if I've got what it takes to really compete, but—"

"I'm sure you—*Biscuit!*" Bev hissed as she spotted a golden tail poking out of Merv's open closet door. She rushed over and found the dog scratching at Merv's collection of blankets. She hoisted him up and turned, flustered, to Merv. "So sorry about that."

"Hm. Are you sure that's a dog, Bev?"

"What else would it be?" she said, walking to the front door and putting him on the other side. "Since you can't behave, you have to sit outside."

His ears drooped as Bev shut the door behind her.

"She says she's not keeping him," Ida said to Merv as she stood near his knitted curtains made from purple, green, and blue yarn. "Did you make these, too? They're lovely."

"I did."

"And what's the material again?"

"Oh, these are from a centicore," he said. "See, it's a bit tougher, but I find it keeps the heat in and the cold out better. Keeps the color longer than some others, so it's good for rugs, too."

"Fascinating!" Ida said with a smile. "Bev, come look at this curtain and quit messing with that dog."

They admired Merv's various creations, and even a novice like Bev had to admit the technique was exquisite.

"I don't know which to submit." If the mole could've blushed, he would have, walking toward the closet that Biscuit had opened and looking at the neatly folded creations. "What sort of things usually win?"

"It varies year to year," Ida said. "But I'd put something up that's an example of your best stitch, has the best quality of yarn, and overall provides an impressive picture." To Bev's quirked brow, she added, "I may have peeked at Petula's book."

"Well, that doesn't make it any easier," Merv said, putting his clawed hands on his hips as he debated, muttering quietly to himself. Finally, he pulled three things from the closet and laid them out as the kettle whistled in the kitchen. "Look at those and tell me which one's the best, will you?"

He waddled to the kitchen while Bev and Ida examined the blankets. "I don't know the first thing about knitting," Bev whispered.

"Me neither," Ida said with a small giggle. "Oh, your dog wants in."

A small nose was visible under the door.

"He can stay out there. Troublemaker," Bev said. "I think this one is quite nice, don't you?"

"Yes, but this one has a prettier color, maybe?" She tutted. "There's a reason I'm not a judge of these things."

"Maybe…" Bev picked up the third, which was the one Biscuit had keyed in on. "Maybe this one?"

"Oh, that one is nice," Ida said with a nod. "Soft, and the stitch is quite complex, don't you think?"

"I was hoping you'd pick that one," Merv said, returning with three cups and a teapot on a serving tray.

Ida's eyes widened at the size of the cups, which were about as large as Bev's mixing bowl for her bread, but she took one with two hands and muttered her thanks. Bev took the other with a smile, and Merv settled on his large chair with the third cup.

"Well? What do you think?"

"I think this one might be the winner," Bev said, putting down the large cup to pick up the purple blanket they'd been admiring. "Unless you feel differently?"

"No, I think that's the one," he said. "But one can never tell these things of their own creation. It's better to hear it from someone else." He smiled—or so Bev assumed, based on the tone of his voice. "So, what else is happening in town?"

~

Bev and Ida stayed as long as was polite, sipping on their tea and informing Merv of the latest events. Not that he really knew who was who in town, but he was interested to hear about the mishaps with the festival, and was positively aghast at the news of Bev's garden.

"But Biscuit did lead me right to it," Bev said with a shrug. "Still haven't a clue who put it there—

or why."

"It was Stanton Bucko," Ida said with a look. "Remember, we found the rosemary sprig in his stuff?"

"We found *a* sprig," Bev said. "Who's to say he didn't cut off a branch and take it for himself before the real culprit destroyed the garden? Besides that, he skipped town already."

She made a face as she brought the cup to her lips. "Oh, Merv, this tea is delicious, but I'm afraid if I drink any more, I might float away."

"Oh, right!" He twitched his whiskers. "I forget you humans are much smaller than I am. Please, don't feel like you have to finish it."

Ida put down her cup with a thankful smile.

"So tell me, there's the fiber arts competition, the bread, and the pies, what other events are there?" Merv asked, sitting back and grabbing his current work in progress and knitting.

Ida stared, mesmerized by his movements, before Bev elbowed her gently. Then she shook herself. "Oh, well, there's jam. The first round happened yesterday, concluding the food preliminaries. Now, we're moving into the handmade goods contests, and there's only one round of that. Quilt-making, embroidery, fiber arts, which includes both crochet and knitted items. There are a few contests for canvas art, too. After that, it's the livestock judging and the most anticipated: the gourds."

Merv let out a chuckle. "Really? Gourds are more important than livestock?"

"Well, the locals have made it that way," Bev said with a smile. "Some fierce competition between the farmers, you know."

"I can only imagine."

"Finally, on the last day of the festival, we have the final round of the food contests, and all the winners get announced," Ida said. "We found it helped people stay in town if we waited until the last day."

"I see."

Bev caught sight of the time on the mantel and put down the large cup. "We've got to get back or we won't get Merv's entry to the judges in time." She gently took the purple blanket from the coffee table. "Hopefully, we'll be back in a few days with a blue ribbon for you."

"Goodness me." Merv all but giggled. "Best not to get an old mole's hopes up, you know?"

They opened the door to leave, but stopped short. Biscuit was fast asleep on the rug, but he woke up immediately and popped to stand as if he'd been ready all along. His tail wagged as he jumped onto Bev's leg, sniffing at the blanket.

"Back off, little monster," Bev said, pulling the

blanket out of harm's way. "I don't know what it is about this thing that he likes. Maybe it just smells weird."

They said their goodbyes and headed back toward the surface. Biscuit remained underfoot more than usual, eager to clamp his little snout into the purple fibers but too short to get there. Bev carried the folded blanket on her shoulder to keep it away from him and hissed at him when he got too close.

"Really, what a strange dog," Ida said. "Maybe you should deposit him back into that forest where you found your garden."

"I tried," Bev said. "He keeps following me."

"Because you keep feeding him."

Bev made a face. It was useless to argue.

Chapter Thirteen

Bev and Ida parted ways when they reached town, Ida taking Merv's blanket to the town hall and Bev and Biscuit heading back toward the inn. For a moment, Bev thought Biscuit might follow Ida and the delicious-smelling blanket, but after a few breaths, he turned and trotted after Bev.

"Was worth a shot," Bev said.

Her good deed for the day done, Bev set to her afternoon chores. The weather was on the warmer side, so she propped the back and front doors open to allow more airflow as she worked in the kitchen. Sometime during the afternoon, Biscuit disappeared from his blanket bed, but she didn't think much of it. Perhaps he'd finally gotten tired of hanging around the inn and found his former master.

Bev popped in to visit Vellora and pick up her daily meat order, hearing another earful from the butcher about her absent wife, and how Vellora was having to do all the work. As before, Bev listened and nodded and didn't say a word about it because it wasn't her business.

Everything was in the oven by mid-afternoon, and the kitchen was preemptively cleaned, so Bev decided to take a turn around the festival to get some fresh air and enjoy one of the last warm days of the season. She once again admired the leather boots, reminding herself she didn't need to spend her gold on something so frivolous, and visited more of the farmers who'd set up shop in the vendor space. Alice had finally brought her baking pumpkins out, and Bev purchased a few to make a soup for the following day, along with some heads of garlic and other things.

"Quite nice to walk to the town square to grab my goods instead of going all the way out to the market," Bev said with a chuckle.

"Nice for you," Alice replied as she handed over the pumpkins. "I still have to lug all this stuff here —and you know there's no room for my wagon."

"True." Bev smiled. "Speaking of pumpkins, the gourd contest is coming up soon, isn't it?"

"Not a moment too soon, if you ask me," Alice said. "Yesterday, I heard yelling from across the fields and saw Herman chasing Trent with a shovel."

"What in the world was Trent doing on your side of town?"

"Scoping out the competition, probably? Who knows. Either way, I'll be happy when they go back to hating each other from a distance."

With her tote heavy with produce, Bev returned to the inn to drop off the gourds. The dog still hadn't returned from whatever mischief he was getting into. She checked her compost pile and Sin's oats and didn't see him anywhere, which was a little odd.

"Not odd, Bev. He probably went home," she replied.

She was about to go sit in the front hall when loud voices echoed from the yard. With a frown, she walked out to see what the commotion was and found Mayor Hendry, Ida, Claude, and Petula arguing as they came up the small side road.

"What's going on?" Bev asked.

"Amateur hour, that's what!" Petula bellowed. "In all my years in the queen's official judging corps, I've never *ever* seen such a poorly managed festival."

"Poorly managed?" Ida gasped. "We've been working our tails off to keep things running smoothly!"

"And this is the first year in twenty that we've had any sort of calamity," Hendry added. "Might I also add it's the first year that it's been *suggested* that we move the festival to another town, and the mayor of that town *happens* to be visiting."

Petula turned to Hendry with a haughty look. "Surely, Jo, you aren't insinuating that the delegation from Middleburg had *anything* to do with this, are you?"

"I'm just stating facts, Petula," Hendry said.

"Hang on," Bev yelled, getting their attention. "What in the world is going on?"

Petula brandished a tattered mess of purple, and Bev's heart sank. Merv's blanket had been thoroughly destroyed, the yarn frayed to the point where it was broken in pieces and unraveling. The only way it was recognizable at all was the unique color.

"Who in the world did this?" Bev shook her head. "And *when*? I thought the main hall was filled with people."

"The when is easy," Ida said. "We'd hung up all the entries in the main hall—as is tradition. We want festivalgoers to be able to see them and admire the work of the artisans in town."

"And destroy it, too!" Petula said.

"Sometime between the initial judging and when the hall reopened," Ida continued, giving the judge a dirty look, "we found Merv's blanket missing. After a quick search, we found it..." She gave Bev a look. "Well, we found it in a forest near your inn, Bev. That's where we were coming from."

"It seems someone's sabotaging our contest entries," Hendry said. "First the pies, now this?"

"Not to mention Bev's garden was destroyed," Ida said.

"Now, that may not be—" Bev began, but she was quickly overruled.

"You know, the only contest that *hasn't* had a misstep was the jams," Hendry continued. "And it's awfully coincidental that every one of the finalists were from Middleburg."

"Jo, come now," Petula said.

"Bev, surely you have something to add," Ida said, her gaze pleading.

"I don't," Bev said, after a long moment—and it was the truth. There was nothing concrete connecting anyone from Middleburg to any of these mishaps. They could all be coincidental, for all she knew.

Hendry and Ida glared at her silence, almost like it was Bev's fault the festival was suffering these mishaps.

"I have to get back to the judging hall," Petula said. "*Hopefully*, there are no more complications with the handmade goods contest. Or any of them!

Because I'm already halfway into writing my report for Her Majesty, and it's not good. You can *rest assured* that if there's one more mess-up, this festival won't be in Pigsend a year longer!"

~

The small crowd dispersed, and Bev returned to the kitchen where Biscuit was sleeping on his mat once more. As she approached, he lifted his head, stretched slowly, and let out a loud yawn.

"What is..." Did she see some purple in his mouth?

Surely not. He was a small dog. How much mischief could a dog his size get into?

Yet as he opened his whole mouth to her in a smile, Bev found a small piece of purple yarn wedged between his teeth. How the heck he'd managed to sneak into the town hall, steal Merv's blanket, and bring it back to his thicket without anyone noticing...she hadn't a clue. But this yarn was too unique to be anything else.

"Oh, buddy. I really wish you hadn't done that." Bev absentmindedly stroked his head. "You need better impulse control."

She sat back, running her hand over her face. She couldn't blame him for *everything*—though she could see a scenario where he'd climbed up on her kitchen table and eaten her rosemary bread, and it was plausible he'd been responsible for destroying her garden. But he hadn't been at the first round of the pie contest—or wait…

"*Did* you knock over the pie table?" Bev asked, looking at him suspiciously.

He'd shown up in her garden *after* that whole fiasco—and he'd actually knocked over one of the tables during the make-up round.

"Whether you're responsible for the pies or not," Bev said, as she stroked his velvety ears, "you're clearly guilty of destroying Merv's blanket. That was a very bad thing you did."

He tilted his head, almost confused.

"Look, I'll cover for you. I won't tell Hendry or Petula or any of them," Bev said. "But you can't… You gotta get out of town before someone else notices you're the problem. Can't say they'll be as nice as I've been."

She put her hand over her eyes, unsure where she could take him. If she locked him in her room for the duration of the festival, he'd howl and whine and scratch—and probably eat her rosemary and everything else he could get his snout into. She obviously couldn't let him run freely. Nor did she think she had the stomach to take him somewhere far from town and dump him. Although she had no question that he would find food, it seemed inhumane. The nights were getting colder, and perhaps she'd become a little used to him sleeping in her bed.

She shook her head. What was she thinking? She couldn't keep him. He had to go.

"Bev? Are you in here?"

Claude came into the kitchen, a bright smile on his face as he held the tattered remains of the purple blanket. Biscuit growled, then lifted his nose in the air and wagged his tail as he trotted toward the blanket.

"Biscuit, back off," Bev said, swatting him away.

"I have fantastic news," Claude said, eyeing Biscuit who'd jumped on his hind legs to reach the blanket.

"Did we find the culprit?"

"Er, no. But I've managed to convince Petula to delay the judging of the contest for a few hours. If we can get another blanket from…this Merv guy, he still has a chance of winning." Claude tilted his head, chewing his lip. "Hopefully? You think?"

"He has a closet full of them, actually," Bev said. "Gave us three to pick from."

"Brilliant!" Claude clapped his hands. "Can we go now?"

Bev glanced at the clock. There were three hours before dinner needed tending to, which gave them plenty of time to pop in and come back. Merv had seemed excited to be included in the contest, although he'd probably be devastated to learn that his hard work had been destroyed by a mischievous little pooch. And Claude, bless him, looked so pleased with himself for convincing Petula to bend the rules a little.

"All right," Bev said, holding her hands up. "I'll head there now."

"Would you...um...mind if I came with you?" Claude asked. "I'd love to meet the man responsible for such artistry. I'm a bit of a knitter myself, and I've never been able to accomplish these kinds of stitches. Maybe he could take me on as an apprentice."

Bev hesitated. Merv was always welcoming, but he probably wouldn't appreciate a steady stream of new people in his house. Still, Claude was responsible for his second chance in the contest.

"Won't Petula have a problem with that?" Bev said. "That seems a bit...biased."

"Well, that was part of the deal to delay the judgment. I said I would recuse myself from the knitted competition if she allowed him entry." He ducked his head, sheepishly. "I thought it was only fair."

"I'm sure he'll appreciate it," Bev said, once more checking the time. "But we'll have to make it a quick visit. Need to be back to make dinner."

There were four muffins left in Allen's basket, so

Bev wrapped them in a tea towel as part of her apology to Merv and put them in a small tote along with the tattered remains of his blanket. Biscuit, unsurprisingly, nosed at the bag, and Bev knocked him back gently with her hip.

"You are *relentless*," she hissed at him.

"He is quite an...intense little dog," Claude said. "Where did you find him?"

"He found me," Bev said with a frown. "And he's caused nothing but trouble since he did."

The trip to Merv's house seemed to go quickly, but perhaps only because Bev was distracted with the question of what to do with the dog. As they passed so-and-so's house, she wondered who would want to take the mischievous creature for a few days. But then Bev imagined herself handing the dog off, telling them to make sure there was no way for him to climb up on tables, hiding food, keeping certain knitted goods away from him, and it seemed like a chaotic mess.

"I think it's very kind that you're so worried about him," Claude said as Bev explained her thoughts. "Especially since you've only had him a few days."

"I wish his owner would show up. But I can see why they're not eager to claim him."

Before she knew it, Bev was rapping at Merv's door, unprepared to explain the situation.

"My, that was quick!" he said with what Bev assumed was a surprised expression. "Did I win?"

"Oh...my goodness..." Claude's eyes had gotten big. "You are..."

"Merv, sorry. This is Claude, one of the judges," Bev said. "Claude, this is Merv."

The poor young man was agape with shock. "N-nice to meet you."

"Bev? Did I win?" Merv pressed.

"Uh, not exactly," Bev said, reaching into her bag. "Look, I'm terribly sorry. There was a mishap with your entry. Um..." She licked her lips as she pulled the remnants of the blanket out. "I'm so sorry."

"What in the world happened to it?" Merv said. "It looks like it was eaten. Did the dog finally get to it?"

Bev chuckled nervously, glancing at Claude. "Why would you say that?"

To her surprise, Merv chuckled. "Because it's the fur of a chimera. Smells interesting to him, I'm sure."

"C-Chimera?" Claude and Bev said at the same time.

"What in the world is that?" Bev asked.

"It's a bit of a mutt in the creature world," Merv said. "This one had the head of a lion and goat, with a snake's tail—obviously, the yarn came from the lion. I got a few skeins from a passing tradesman a few years ago and made the blanket. Difficult to work with, won't do that again for sure." He chuckled as he knelt toward Biscuit. "And you, little one, are full of curiosity."

"The judges have allowed you another entry, if you want," Bev said, nodding at Claude, who'd been hanging on Merv's every word. "Right, Claude?"

"Oh, right. Yes! Of course." He nodded quickly. "Provided that we get it in the next hour or two."

"Well, I've got a couple more options to share with you. Come with me."

Without fail, Biscuit bounded between Bev's legs and made a beeline for the open closet. Bev made a noise, but Merv held up his hand.

"It's fine. It's what they do." He opened the door and patted Biscuit on the head. "Let's see what else I have."

Bev heaved a sigh of relief that Merv didn't seem bothered by Biscuit's antics. Claude seemed enraptured by Merv's kitchen, and since Merv didn't say anything, Bev figured it was all right for the young judge to roam.

"You certainly do have a stubborn streak, don't you?" Merv said, gently moving a blanket out of reach of the dog.

"I don't know what I'm going to do with him,"

Bev said, lowering her voice so Claude wouldn't hear. "He's a bundle of trouble and relentless. Scented something from across the street and broke into a house where one of the pie makers was staying. I found him snout-deep in...." She glanced at Claude puttering around the kitchen and decided against mentioning the barus bauble. "...baking materials."

"Seriously?" Claude said, poking his head out of the kitchen. "What was he doing in there?"

"Her pie filling was irresistible, I suppose," Bev said with a look to Merv. "But keeping him out of trouble is next to impossible when all these other mishaps are happening."

The mole nodded slowly. "And you suspect he might be the cause."

She winced, nodding toward the kitchen, but Claude didn't show any indication he'd heard that, as he was inspecting Merv's collection of teas.

"I'm worried if I bring him back to town, he'll do something else and the whole of Pigsend will be out for him. The mayor's already nervous that the festival's going to get sent to another town. I don't know what she'd do to him if she found out he was responsible."

"Mm." Merv pulled out a blanket. "Why don't you let him stay here until the festival's over? I'm sure he'd be happy here."

Bev eyed him. "Are you...joking? He's a menace."

"Oh, he's curious. I'm sure we can come to an agreement while he stays here." He handed her a green blanket, not quite as intricate as the purple one, but soft as silk. "This one. What do you think?"

Bev glanced at the clock. She didn't have time to argue. "It's perfect. And if you're sure about keeping the dog here…"

"Quite. I think it'll be nice to have some company," he said. "After all, how much of a menace can he be?"

Chapter Fourteen

Bev and Claude returned to town in the nick of time. Claude handed the blanket over to Petula, who huffed as she disappeared inside the town hall, muttering about special circumstances and amateur judges. But they'd made the cut-off, and Merv's blanket was included in the competition. And when Bev arrived back at the inn, the clock struck five— time to pull dinner from the oven.

As she plated everything up, her gaze kept drifting toward Biscuit's makeshift bed on the floor. She should've probably picked the sheet up, put it in the basket to be washed. But she kept walking by it, leaving it where it was, actually missing the little demon who'd somehow crawled into her heart and made a mess there.

But it was for the best. She served dinner and learned that the handmade contest had gone off without a hitch from Claude, who brought Merv's entry back to her to return to him.

"Petula's asked Sheriff Rustin to stand guard in the town hall overnight, just to make sure no one does anything funny to the competition space," he said, helping himself to another piece of bread. "I don't know what mischief anyone would cause in an empty room, but he agreed to it."

Bev chuckled. Rustin would surely be fast asleep in his office by now. "That's good to hear. What about the other soldiers?"

"They've been set to watch the pasture outside town. All the showing animals have been put there overnight so we can start the livestock judging first thing in the morning," he said with a heavy sigh. "This judging thing is a lot more stressful than I thought it would be."

Bev nodded. "You sound like you could use another ale."

"I would if I drank," he said with a chuckle. "You've probably gone through several casks of it this week, I'd wager."

"The Harvest Festival clears my stash, for sure," Bev said. "But it's a nice winter project to brew more for the spring. Things tend to get really quiet in town once the snow starts falling."

"I'm sure that'll be welcome, after all the frenzy." He sighed, looking out in the room. "You know, getting that second entry for Merv...it was the right thing to do—no matter what Petula thought."

"I agree." She glanced at the fireplace, looking for the dog again. "Hopefully, Biscuit is doing well at Merv's."

"Merv seemed to find his chaotic attentions charming." Claude paused and turned to Bev. "Where did you—pardon my pun—dig up Merv, anyway?"

"He and I met during the sinkhole fiasco," Bev said. "The earthquakes were damaging his home. But he seems to have put everything back together."

"I'm glad. He seems like a kind soul."

He was kind, but would Merv have enough potato skins for Biscuit to be satisfied? Would he know... She stopped herself before she went down that path. If he stayed at the inn, the temptation to get into trouble would be too strong.

"I'm sure the dog is fine," Claude said to Bev's silence. "Not that I know much about them, but there's not much to make them happy."

"But you must know a lot about dogs, right? Your aunt has a pack of them, last I spoke with her,"

Bev said. "They're her pride and joy."

"And that's how I know they don't like me," he said with a quick smile. "I'm going to go sit and eat, if you want to—"

"Oh, of course, of course." Bev shooed him away. "Go eat. Sorry to talk your ear off."

Bev busied herself with checking on the diners, refilling tankards of ale, and asking how they were enjoying the festival. Unlike the night before, she was quite pleased with how dinner had come out, so she was eager to hear the feedback. Of course, even with the garlic, the bread wasn't devoured as quickly as usual, but at least there weren't any large pieces left.

The crowd was dwindling when the front door opened and two people barged in loudly—Felicia Dinwight and Mayor Twinsly.

Bev plastered on a smile as she turned to them, her hand on her hip. "I'm not sure there's much food left," she said. "Dinner's been on for a few hours, but—"

"Forget that, you...you...cretin!" Felicia howled.

The whole dining room went silent.

Bev blinked. "I'm sorry, what?"

"You and that mayor of yours. You're out to get me!"

"Calm down, Ms. Dinwight," Petula said,

coming to stand beside her.

Bev winced a little; she'd hoped the judge had already gone to bed. Claude, too, came up to see what the fuss was about.

"Now tell us what happened," Petula said patiently.

"My pie-making materials are *gone*," she snarled, pointing at Bev. "And this...this...this saboteur is responsible!"

"Why would I take your pie-making materials?" Bev asked with a roll of her eyes. "I'm not a pie-maker, nor do I want to be."

"You were in my room the other day. Explain that!"

Petula's beady eyes swept toward Bev, and warmth climbed her neck. Luckily, she did have the truth on her side. "I was trying to find Bisc—that little dog's owner. He got loose and managed to sneak into Lazlo's house where Felicia is staying."

"I find that *highly unlikely*." Felicia sniffed.

"The back door was open," Bev said with a shrug. "I'm not sure what he scented in your room that made him so excited, but when I found him, he was nose-deep in your things." She paused, blinking. "What, exactly, has gone missing?"

Felicia opened and closed her mouth, glancing at Petula—and that was all Bev needed to know. Someone had taken her barus bauble. Of course, she couldn't say that outright (perhaps she hadn't thought through this storming-into-the-inn-and-causing-a-scene plan).

"Well, Ms. Dinwight, what's gone missing?" Petula prompted.

"My jar of strawberry-rhubarb filling," she said, after working her jaw. "And it's the only one I have for the contest."

"And when did it go missing?"

"I checked it this afternoon at five. When I returned to my house, it was gone!"

"It couldn't have been me," Bev said with a smile. "I've been here serving food." She gestured to the room. "We got back from Merv's at around five, didn't we, Claude?"

For a moment, he looked like he was going to disagree with her, but then he emphatically nodded. "I can vouch for that."

"Then your damn dog," Felicia said. "Where is he?"

"He's at Merv's," Bev said, her heart sinking a little as she said it. "Because he was getting into too much trouble around here, I thought it best to send him elsewhere until the festival's concluded."

Felicia huffed and puffed. "Well, then...*who did it*?"

"Perhaps you misplaced your wares," Petula said. "But I don't think it's very becoming to barge in here with unfounded accusations. Especially you, Mayor Twinsly."

The mayor had been watching silently. "I don't think it's coincidence that a person in both the pie *and* bread-maker competitions was targeted."

"Were any of your bread-making materials stolen?" Petula asked.

Again, Felicia hesitated. Bev had a feeling the barus bauble was being used for both. "No."

"It seems there are many accusations going around," Petula said. "Some have been leveled in your direction as well, Miranda."

The mayor twitched. "Jo Hendry is paranoid. Nobody's ruining her festival but her own shoddy management."

"Let's put a pin in this," Petula said, holding up her hands. "Everyone go back to your meals. In the morning, we can have a chat about your missing pie contents and see what we can do about it."

It seemed the crowd wanted to discuss it further, but they adhered to Petula's guidance, dispersing and moving back to their respective dinners. Twinsly and Felicia took the longest to leave, but once they did, Bev returned to her seat behind the counter, a new idea stuck in her mind.

She'd chalked Biscuit's mischievous nature up to being a dog without much impulse control. But what if there was something *more*? Merv had had his doubts that the creature was a dog at all—what had he called him? A leaderloo? It definitely started with an l…

With a cursory glance out to the patrons, many still discussing the dramatic scene they'd witnessed, Bev snuck upstairs to her room. She quickly inspected her rosemary plant in the window—it still didn't look like it had grown any—next to the amulet piece in her top drawer—still there.

Then she knelt and lifted a loose floorboard, revealing a small treasure trove of gold and a book.

Back during the sinkhole debacle, Bev had borrowed this encyclopedia of magical creatures from the library. The old librarian had never asked for it back, so Bev had stashed it under her bed.

There wasn't much light to read in here, so she headed downstairs with the book under her arm and walked directly into the kitchen. She placed the book on her kitchen table and flipped through the pages. Each creature was accompanied by a drawing and a short description, though some had more detail than others. Bev passed the entries on barus and gnomes, which had been essential in dealing with those magical creatures the month before.

She reached the "L" creatures and slowed, trying to remember what Merv had called Biscuit. Then she found a drawing resembling a dog.

LAELAPS

The laelaps is a magical-detector creature, one of many different kinds. Intensely loyal, they bond immediately with a familiar (usually a magical human) and help locate magic in the surrounding environment using their keen sense of smell. But unlike other magical detectors, for example guillens, they act more as a scout than a destroyer, alerting their familiar of its presence.

Laelaps are easily confused with the common dog and may roam with packs for their own safety. But they are most obviously identified by their trademark golden eyes.

The drawing was of a tall, thin dog—nothing like Mr. Biscuit. Yet the golden eyes were a dead ringer. He'd certainly got the loyalty thing down, too, though Bev wasn't magical so that didn't quite fit. But maybe Merv wasn't too far off in thinking there was more to the little dog than met the eye.

She glanced at the window, where the remnants of her herb garden were still hanging to dry. There was...perhaps a reasonable assumption that her herbs did have some latent magic in them, albeit unknowingly on Bev's part. She still couldn't quite see how Biscuit could've uprooted all the plants and taken them to the small thicket, but he'd definitely *found* them.

Then, there was the bauble. He'd been able to scent *that* from inside Felicia's bag across the street.

Merv's blanket was magical, though again, mostly latent. Bev did have a quibble with the book's assertion that laelaps weren't destructive. Clearly, Biscuit had missed that particular trait.

So her mischievous dog was merely a creature with an innate need to find magical things. And he was finding things that weren't *supposed* to be magical.

Bev rubbed her face, glancing at his empty spot near the kitchen fireplace. A magical sniffer wouldn't be the worst thing to have around, provided he learned how to behave himself and *signal* instead of—

"What am I saying?" Bev said to no one. "He can't stay here."

"Who can't stay here?" Mayor Hendry let herself into the kitchen. "What have you found?"

"Nothing, Jo," Bev replied, closing the book. "Nothing related to the festival."

"Are you sure? Because I saw Twinsly looking positively *livid* this evening. You didn't find anything?"

"She was mad because one of her pie-makers seems to have misplaced the magical object they were using to cheat," Bev said, putting the book on the lower shelf of her table.

"Hang on, *you found a magical object*?" Hendry practically leapt over the table. "And you didn't tell me? Or Petula?"

"My... The dog did," Bev said. "I decided to keep it mum because it would raise too many questions. I'm not in the business of getting anyone arrested for using illegally procured magic." She glared at Hendry. "Because that would be the result."

Hendry made a face, and Bev had a feeling the mayor wouldn't shed a tear if her nemesis was hauled away in chains.

"All I want is for whoever's messing up this festival to stop," Hendry said after a moment.

"I'm reasonably confident I've found the culprit," Bev said. "And they won't be causing any more trouble."

"Okay, then who was it?"

"The dog," Bev said. "I think he's a magical sniffer called a laelaps, and he's been drawn to all the cheaters in the festival. Or unintentional magic users, like Merv."

Hendry blinked. "Are you...serious? The *dog*."

"Of course I'm serious." Bev explained the various places she'd seen him, but Hendry's expression didn't change.

"That's a stretch, Bev."

"Well, he's with Merv now," Bev said. "So we'll see if there are any more unfortunate events. If not, then we can be confident that I've found the culprit."

Hendry pursed her lips. "If a *dog's* been behind all this, we should find out who brought him. Probably Miranda."

Bev chuckled. "Look, I've been all over the village looking for his owner, and nobody's come forward to claim him. So maybe he wandered into town with the rest of the travelers and decided to hang out near my garden."

Hendry paused, eyeing her. "You said he's attracted to magic? Is there magic in your garden?"

Bev paused, schooling her expression. She trusted Hendry, but not that much. "Petula seemed to think so. If there is, it's not by my doing. But as Karolina and her team informed us, there's magic in the ground all over this place."

"Indeed. And it would explain the *draw* of your rosemary bread," Hendry said.

"Probably should consider pulling out of the contest, then," Bev said, turning to walk away. "Since I've got an unfair advantage—"

"Absolutely *not*," Hendry bellowed. "You will submit the best bread and you *will* win a blue ribbon, do you hear?" She straightened. "And I don't want to hear another word about it."

"Very well, I—"

A loud commotion came from the dining room, and Bev and Hendry walked out to investigate. Petula's two soldiers were in hurried conversation with her, looking like they'd run there.

"What's going on?" Hendry said, sounding almost afraid to find out.

"We've left the pasture where the show animals are being kept," Ridge Holt said, his eyes wide. "Someone…someone left open the back gate, and they've all escaped."

CHAPTER FIFTEEN

Bev followed Hendry, Petula, and the rest of those gathered in the inn to the pasture that Earl Dollman had set up outside town. He was there in conversation with Ida, Claude, and Mayor Twinsly, who wore a look of superiority as they talked.

"To my eyes, nothing's broken," he said. "The gate latch is solid. Nobody's done a thing to it except, well...leave it open."

"And yet here we are. A pasture with zero animals," Twinsly said, glancing at Hendry. "Another *stellar* performance, Jo."

"He said it wasn't broken, *Miranda*," Hendry said. "Clearly, *someone* left the gate open."

"Who was the last one here?" Petula asked. "Ridge? Marcelano?"

The two soldiers looked sheepishly at the ground. "Well, we were both here. But..." Ridge began.

"But I guess..."

"I suppose..."

"Out with it," Petula barked.

"It's like...they disappeared," Ridge said. "Like...um..."

"Magic?" Bev prompted.

"Well, obviously not *magic*," Petula said with a shake of her head. "Because that would be in direct conflict with Her Majesty's edicts about magical use. And there's no one with an approved magic license in town, is there?"

Bev glanced around the group. In the mix, she counted at least two—Hendry and Ida—who had innate magic, and perhaps three more who *might* have some kind of magical abilities. But nobody made a peep.

"That's what I thought," Petula said with a huff. "Therefore, it's clear I need to write you both up for dereliction of duty."

They hung their heads. Bev didn't know what that meant for those in the queen's service, but based on their expressions, it wasn't good.

"And in the meantime, we need to find the

livestock before someone else does," Petula barked. "The longer we stand around pointing fingers, the farther they'll be able to roam."

"How many animals are we talking about?" Bev asked Ida, who had her trusty clipboard.

"Ten cows, fifteen pigs, twenty sheep, eighteen goats, and twelve rabbits," Ida counted.

"How the heck did the rabbits get out?" cried one of those gathered. "They were in an enclosed pen!"

"The same way all the others did, I'd wager," Twinsly said, giving a death glare to Hendry, who returned it. "Someone clearly wanted to sabotage the livestock showing tomorrow. And considering *most* of those in the contest were from Middleburg —"

"Unless *someone* wanted to make Pigsend look bad by releasing the animals," Hendry shot back.

"Will you two *cut it out*?" Petula barked. "In all my years of judging, I've never encountered two politicians who act so immaturely. Whatever bad blood exists between you two needs to be set aside."

"Since there are so many animals to find," Claude said, "we should find more volunteers to search. Mayor Hendry, do you think you could round up people from town?"

"Of *course*," Hendry replied. "Pigsend is more than happy to work together."

"I'll be sure to call on the Middleburg delegation," Twinsly replied. "They're *always* eager to help out those less fortunate."

"I swear to…" Petula muttered. "Fine. Call the whole town if you want. But those who are here, *get moving.*"

~

Word had already spread about the livestock being released, and a good number of Pigsend residents showed up near the pasture to form a search party. Hendry counted them off to Ida, who wrote down their names as she divvied them up into groups and sent them out into the night. When Twinsly returned with the Middleburg delegation, also sizable, Hendry very loudly said they weren't needed.

"You can return to your homes," she said. "We've got this covered."

"We don't," Claude said. "Let's take all the help we can get."

Hendry scowled at the young judge, and Ida wrote down their names, divvying them up into groups and sending them on their way.

"Where do you want me to look?" Bev asked.

"I don't know what else is left," she said, putting her hand on her forehead as she scanned the list. "But maybe you and Hendry can go somewhere else because she's getting on my ever-loving *nerves.*"

Indeed, the mayor had let out a loud *whoop* of celebration when the first Pigsend search party came back with two cows.

"You see?" Hendry cried. "Don't send strangers to look in our town. We know where to look."

She seemed to regret her celebration when a Middleburg search party brought back three goats and Twinsly made sure Ida *wrote that down.*

"Wait a minute," Bev said. "You said you found the goats down by Eldred's place, right?"

They nodded. "That's where you told us to look, so that's where we went."

"That's on the polar opposite side of town from where the cows were found," Bev said to Ida. "How strange that they would travel so far so quickly."

More search parties came back with different animals found in different corners of town. Petula had said there couldn't have been magic afoot, but in Bev's experience, livestock didn't move that fast —except for maybe the goats. It was another curiosity, another question to unravel as to who was actually behind the chaos in town.

"I swear to… *It's not a contest,*" Ida barked when both Twinsly and Hendry asked her who'd found more livestock. "The most important thing is that we *find* them all in time for tomorrow's competition. In case you ladies forgot, these animals actually *belong* to people."

"I didn't forget," Twinsly insisted.

"You absolutely did—"

"Hey, Jo," Bev said, as Hendry looked ready to attack. "Why don't you go search down by Pigsend Creek? Maybe some of the animals wanted a drink."

"And Miranda can go look up by the dark forest," Ida said, knowing that Hendry wouldn't argue with that destination.

"Fine," they said in unison then seemed annoyed they'd done *anything* together.

"Thank you," Ida whispered.

"But only if Bev comes with me," Hendry said.

"Fine, I'll go," Bev said without missing a beat.

"Be sure to come back and let me know, even if you don't find anything," Ida called as they split up.

~

It might've been a good time to have a dog around, even if that dog was a mischievous laelaps. Bev had her glowing stick, but she seemed to be the only one actually keeping an eye out for any of the animals. Hendry was too busy talking (very loudly) about how ridiculously Twinsly was acting.

"You can *tell* she knew what happened," Hendry said. "Absolutely obvious on her face. She wants to destroy our festival by any means necessary. It's a good thing Petula's starting to see through her tricks." She smirked. "I wouldn't be surprised if an inquiry was opened into Middleburg's management.

The queen herself might step in and remove the mayor."

"For upending the Harvest Festival?" Bev asked. "Seems like an extreme reaction."

"Well, a gal can dream."

"Why don't we keep our voices down," Bev said. "We might be scaring away the livestock."

"Bev, this is on the opposite side of town," Hendry said. "I doubt we'll find anything over here."

"Won't we?" Bev walked to another thick bush and peered inside. "The animals seem to be spread to the four winds. That's awfully fishy."

"Animals move."

"Yes, but either the soldiers were asleep on the job for...well, *hours*, which doesn't make sense because Claude and Petula didn't come to dinner until seven. Or someone with some magic moved the animals." She rubbed her chin. "But why?"

"Because they—"

"What if it had nothing to do with the festival?" Bev said.

"Of *course* it had something to do with the festival."

"But what if it didn't? What does that change?"

Hendry sighed, watching Bev for a moment before responding. "I know that, for whatever reason, you like to see the best in people. But in this case, we know the Middleburg folks *are* cheating with magic. You saw it yourself. So, it's reasonable to assume they were also responsible for releasing all the animals so Petula will move the festival."

It was reasonable, and yet, Bev couldn't help but think there was more to the story.

"You said that...uh...dog of yours seems sensitive to magic, no?" Hendry said.

"Not my dog anymore," Bev said.

"Maybe you should get him back. Might help your investigation."

"How come I always end up investigating the problems in town?" Bev asked. "Why not get Rustin to handle it?"

"Darling, he's *far* too...busy."

"If you say so," Bev said, taking her glowing stick over to a dark clump of bushes and pushing them aside. Nothing. "But it's not in my job description to solve mysteries."

"It seemed to be with those sinkholes."

"Because..." Bev let out a frustrated noise. "Look. Next time something weird happens in town, *leave me out of it*. Got it?"

She lifted her shoulder and kept walking.

Bev glared at her but was grateful for the silence so she could listen for anything stirring in the darkness. They walked the length of the road, down close to Trent Scrawl's property where some of the sinkhole drama had taken place.

"Who do you think's going to win, Trent or Herman?" Hendry asked.

"Haven't really paid attention to their gourds," Bev replied, taking her glowing stick over to more thickets and pushing them aside. "But I know Alice is ready for it to be over."

"Mm. Does make for a fun contest though. We should have more rivalries. It might draw more people."

"We have plenty of people in town for the festival. Can't house them all as it is. Isn't that one of the strikes against us?" Bev said, crossing the street to look on the other side. Nothing.

"What if you expanded the inn?"

"I'll get right on that with all the gold I have hoarded in my shoe," Bev said. "Near cleaned me out to get the front of the inn repaired. Good thing those soldiers coughed up some money."

"Then I could invite someone to build another inn somewhere in the city."

"Fine by me," Bev said, annoyed with the conversation. Why couldn't Hendry leave well enough alone? The festival was fine at the size it was, even with the mishaps this year. Any larger and it would spill out of the town limits. If anything, she was inadvertently making the argument for it to be moved to Middleburg.

"How much farther are we planning to walk?" Hendry said with a loud sigh. "My feet hurt."

"I was going to go all the way to Sonny's Mill," Bev said, turning. "But we can head back if you want. I haven't seen as much as a hoofprint out this way. Hopefully, when we get back it'll be—"

A loud sound echoed through the darkness. Hendry let out an uncharacteristically high-pitched squeal of terror as she jumped toward Bev.

Bev held her breath as she lifted the glowing stick higher. "Hello?"

A beat. Then a *bleat*.

Bev's entire body relaxed. "A goat. Looks like there was something out this far after all." Hendry hadn't moved. "Are you going to help or not?"

"I'm not touching that thing," Hendry said with a frown. "It's filthy. And probably smells like a barnyard."

"That's because it lives in a..." Bev shook her head. "Are you telling me you searched for animals with no intention of bringing them back?"

"Why do you think I came with you? I'm not stupid."

Luckily, the goat had a collar and tag, so Bev guided the animal back toward the larger enclosure. She half-expected Hendry to peel off and head back to her house, but perhaps the mayor wanted to be seen as the hero, even though she'd done...exactly nothing to help.

A crowded pen welcomed the trio when they finally reached the pasture outside town.

Ida's face lit up in a relieved smile as she checked the clipboard. "That's the last goat," she said. "Thank goodness."

Hendry peered over Ida's shoulder at her clipboard. "How many did—"

"I stopped counting, Jo," Ida said with a look. "Everybody did their part. Hooray."

"Is everything back?" Bev asked.

"Let me check." She ran her finger down the pages then frowned. "No. I'm missing one pig."

"I'm not going to look for it," Hendry said. "It's past midnight."

"It's a Middleburg pig," Ida said, almost daring her to change her mind.

"Then Twinsly can find it." Hendry yawned. "I'm going home."

And before either of them could argue, she was halfway down the road.

"How many more search parties are out there?" Bev asked.

"None. You guys were the last," Ida said, letting out a yawn herself. "I really don't feel like going back out again. Vellora's already probably furious I didn't come home for dinner or to help clean the shop tonight. But it couldn't be avoided. Some of these farmers are our best customers."

"I'm sure she'll understand," Bev said, though she had a feeling Vellora wouldn't. "Look, it's late. There's nothing more we can do tonight. In the morning, we'll head back out and look again. I'm sure it'll turn up eventually."

"Hopefully," Ida said. "Or Petula Banks is going to have my head."

"After she finishes with the soldiers on duty, I hope," Bev said. "They were the ones supposed to be watching things. Not you."

"No, but, somehow...somehow all these mishaps end up on my shoulders as a committee member," she said. "I'm not getting paid enough for this. I'm not getting paid *anything* for this."

Bev could relate. "Let's get home. This will all look better in the morning."

They walked together in silence, only saying goodbye when they parted ways. But as Bev walked through the front door of the inn, her plans of falling headfirst into bed were dashed, as there was a large someone sitting in the chair by the fireplace.

"Merv, what are you—" Bev began but the mole man jumped to his feet before she could finish.

"Bev, I'm so sorry, but this...*whatever he is*...is a menace!"

CHAPTER SIXTEEN

Bev's gaze immediately searched the room for Biscuit, and she found him sprawled out in front of the fireplace, fast asleep. But at Merv's loud bellow, he woke up, growled at the fire then seemed to notice Bev. His entire body shifted as his tail began thumping on the ground and that trademark smile spread across his snout. He trotted happily over to Bev and nuzzled her leg, and she couldn't help but give him a welcome scratch behind the ears.

"What happened?" Bev asked, although she had a pretty good idea already.

"I tried my best to keep him at my place, but he destroyed everything and spent the entire time whining at the door." Merv gestured to the air with his long claws. "My ears hurt, and I'm exhausted trying to keep him out of everything. He won't listen to a word I say. Practically bounded back here when I let him out of my house. I think he wants to be with you."

Biscuit's tail was wagging so fast it wasn't visible anymore, and he kept trying to lick Bev's hands hanging by her side.

"I'm so sorry, Merv. Really," Bev said after a long moment. "I shouldn't have left him with you."

"No, no, I insisted. Silly of me to think I could keep a laelaps from their familiar," Merv said with a shake of his head.

"Do you...know much about laelaps?" Bev asked. "I have some light reading about them, but nothing substantial."

"They've got the best magical sniffers around," he said. "Can track a magical object from miles away, even. Loyal, too, that checks out. But they're also supposed to be highly intelligent which..." He cast his small eyes toward the dog, who had started circling the room sniffing the floor. "That's up for debate. He's either very intelligent and very keen to get what he wants, or he's just a klutzy fool."

"Maybe a little of both," Bev said as Biscuit knocked over the fireplace kit with a loud crash and, unfazed, kept sniffing the floor. "I'm sorry you had to come all the way out here to bring him—and so late."

"I would've come earlier, but you know how I despise the sun," he said. "Where have you been, though? I've been waiting for hours."

Bev told him about the livestock being set free, and how they'd spent all night searching for them.

Merv shook his head. "More than a few hiccups. And this one, you can't blame on the laelaps."

"No, I guess I can't," Bev said, scratching Biscuit's ears. Was she actually...excited to have him back? She couldn't help the smile on her lips as he leaned into her pets. "Suppose we'll have to find the real culprit. My new theory is someone in town has a great deal of magic. Maybe in the Middleburg delegation, but maybe not."

"Good thing you have a magical sniffer to help," Merv said. "Now if you'll excuse me, I've got a journey to get back home."

"Oh!" Bev only remembered that Allen had returned Merv's blanket and ran to retrieve it from the back of the room. "I thought you might want this one back."

He held up his large claws. "No, no. Please. I insist you keep it. And I hope to hear from you after the festival is over. Maybe you can stay for a cuppa." He paused. "But you know, leave the laelaps at home next time."

Bev walked Merv out and saw him off before turning back to the mischievous little dog sitting by her feet. He was awfully well-behaved at the moment, sticking close to her and not going very far. She closed the front door behind her, and they walked through the front room.

"I can't say I didn't miss you," she said. "Are you hungry?"

He opened his mouth in a smile.

"Who am I kidding? You're always hungry. Let's see what I can find."

Bev walked into the kitchen and let out a low groan. It was an absolute *mess,* and she didn't have the energy to tackle the mountain of dishes tonight.

"You know," she said, walking to the bucket of potato skins on the ground and dumping them out for Biscuit to gobble up, "you could grow some thumbs and help me clean up around here every once in a while instead of eating my garbage."

He ate, and Bev scrubbed a few dishes, putting a few more in a bath of lye and water to ease the load in the morning. She let out another sigh when she considered how busy she'd be tomorrow. Find a missing pig, bake some bread, get dinner squared away, maybe even do a wash of her tunics...

"Yeah, it would be nice if you could help out," Bev said, looking at Biscuit. "Or at least find that pig."

He looked up as if understanding her. But no, he wanted to go out to relieve himself as he trotted to the back door and sat expectantly.

"Okay, okay." Bev walked to the door and opened it. "But make it—hey!"

Biscuit shot out the door and disappeared into the night.

The last thing she wanted to be doing at one in the morning was following her dog (*laelaps, whatever*) through the dark, but something told her she should. Based on his direction, she was pretty sure she knew where he was headed, which also made her more curious.

The small thicket where he'd seemed to hoard all his treasures was up ahead, and Bev held her breath, worried what she'd find inside. Biscuit, of course, zipped through the underbrush while Bev was stuck pushing through the branches and brambles.

Biscuit began barking excitedly, and Bev thought she heard a voice.

"Hello?" Bev called and immediately regretted it. What if Biscuit had led her to the mysterious magic user? They probably didn't want Bev barging in on their magical doings. She stopped, listening for the sound of the voice again, and when she heard nothing except Biscuit's loud brays, she pressed on.

There was something ahead, and when Bev pulled the last branch out of the way, she let out a gasp of surprise.

"It's…the missing pig."

Or so Bev assumed—why else would a pig be hanging around a forest thicket in the middle of the night? She drew closer and found the telltale collar around its neck, marking it as one of the showing animals. The voice must've been the pig's excited squeal from seeing a dog show up out of nowhere.

Biscuit was sniffing around its hindquarters, his tail wagging excitedly as the pig snorted and sniffed at the ground.

"Good boy, Biscuit," she said, half amazed that he'd done…well, exactly as she'd asked him.

Maybe there was something to this laelaps-familiar thing that Merv was talking about.

"Let's go home," Bev said. "Help me get this pig moving."

That was easier said than done as the pig was about as stubborn as Biscuit and refused to move. Bev had to get behind him and shove him forward to get him moving, and even once he was mobile, he kept stopping every few feet. Biscuit, bless him, nipped and growled at the pig's back legs like a cattle dog herding sheep, but the pig was slow-moving.

"You know," Bev huffed as she once again got

behind him to push him forward, "for someone who traveled so far, you're awfully hard to move."

Eventually, they found a slow but steady gait through the middle of town toward the pasture. Bev kept glancing at the pig for any signs that it was somehow...not really a pig. Much like Biscuit being mistaken for a dog, it was plausible this animal was really something else. Biscuit had found him quickly, and if he was a magical sniffer, he would've been drawn to him.

Or, perhaps, Bev had asked her laelaps to do a job, he'd done it, and there was absolutely nothing special about this creature, other than its stubbornness. Biscuit certainly didn't seem interested in it now other than to move it along.

"Just a pig," Bev said to herself.

A pig who stopped abruptly again in the middle of the road.

"Come *on,* you little..." Bev grunted as she assumed the position again. "Not much farther. Tons of mud for you to roll around it. Food too!" She pushed. "Just...a...little...farther..."

The pig took a step forward, and Bev fell flat on her face.

"B-Bev?"

Bev looked up into the concerned gazes of Claude and Ridge. "Good evening, gentlemen."

"I take it you found the last pig," Ridge said,

reaching down to help her up.

Biscuit growled ominously, and Bev shushed him. "Be nice."

The growling stopped, but the dog still looked wary of the two men.

"It's my fault," Claude said, backing up a step nervously. "I told you, dogs hate me."

"He's not a… Anyway." Bev didn't feel like explaining. "Yes. We found the last pig now. And if he'd move a little faster, maybe we could all go to bed."

The pig let out a loud snort.

"Were you two out looking for him?" Bev asked. "I thought Ida told everyone to go home."

"She did, but I felt so bad," Ridge said. "I swear, I didn't see a darn thing. We don't even know how long they'd been out. Thought they'd gotten so quiet because they'd all gone to sleep." He was babbling now, and Bev couldn't help noticing how young he seemed—maybe the same age as Claude.

"It's all right, Ridge," Claude said. "These things happen. I promise, I'll send a letter along with Petula that'll vouch for you."

"Surely, their punishment won't be too severe," Bev said, looking between the two of them. "It was an honest mistake." Or, more likely, the actions of someone with a nefarious goal in mind.

"No, once we return to the capital, we'll

probably be sacked—or worse." He lifted a shoulder. "Her Majesty doesn't like failure. Perfection at all levels was drilled into our minds from the moment we started training." He sighed. "I hope it's not thirty days..."

"Of what?" Bev blinked. "Surely not jail."

"Let's not discuss unpleasant things," Claude said. "Look, why don't you take the pig to the pasture, Ridge, and Bev and I can walk back to the inn, hm? It's been a long night for us all."

Bev wasn't about to argue with him. "Here. All yours."

"Thank you." He took the pig by the collar. "You really saved my, uh..." He grinned. "Bacon?"

"Har har." Bev turned to go with Claude. "Have a good night. We'll see you in the morning."

~

"You seemed awfully invested in getting the livestock back," Bev said as she and Claude walked back to the inn. "Thought you said you didn't care for that part of the contest."

"And you seem to have your dog back," Claude replied with a smile as Biscuit kept his distance with his lip curled up in a silent snarl. "I thought he was with Merv."

"He was, but, uh..." Bev laughed. "Well, let's say it wasn't a good fit."

Claude laughed. "That's an understatement.

Couldn't believe that mole wanted to take him. Anyone could've seen that mistake from a mile away."

"Merv's got this sunny sort of optimism," Bev said. "It's part of why I like him so much. That, and he tends to know a lot of things about..." She decided against finishing her original thought. No matter how nice Claude was, it wasn't prudent to discuss magic and magical items with a stranger. "Hospitality. And tea."

"He did have a nice collection," Claude said. "And the handmade goods were phenomenal."

"You never did get a chance to ask him to teach you, did you?" Bev said with a sigh. "Well, if you hang around after the festival is over, maybe you can pay him another visit with me."

"Leave the dog at home, though, right?"

"That's what Merv said," Bev said, glancing down at Biscuit, whose hair was still standing on end as if Claude were a dangerous viper. "Biscuit, calm down, buddy. Boy, you weren't kidding about dogs not liking you."

"It's a curse, I swear."

"Well, I'll keep him out of your hair until the festival's over," Bev said. "Gotta keep him out of everyone's hair, that's for sure."

"But you're still looking for his owner, right?"

Bev honestly wasn't so sure. "If someone shows

up claiming ownership, I'd be happy to hand him over. Whether he'd go is another story. He's somewhat attached to me now."

"Clearly," Claude said, glancing at him. "He hasn't been more than two steps away from you this whole walk back."

"I'm glad I don't have to get up and search for that pig again," Bev said as the inn came into view. "It's already going to be a long morning, what with the late hour tonight and the mess in the kitchen. I'll be lucky if I get everything done before noon."

"Must be tough running things all by yourself," Claude said.

"Not nearly as tough as working for the queen." She shook her head. "Thirty days in jail for a small mistake like that? Seems overly harsh."

"I don't pretend to know the details," he said. "But there's a reason the queen won and the king didn't."

They passed the butcher shop. Had Vellora had yelled at Ida for being late? "So I've been told."

He shook his head. "I find it fascinating you have *no* memory of anything beyond five years ago."

Bev lifted a shoulder. "There's probably a good reason I don't. Digging to find more would lead to a whole bunch of trouble I don't have time for."

"To my eyes, it seems trouble finds you," Claude said as she opened the front door. "Thank you. I suppose I'll see you in the morning? If you need a hand in the kitchen—"

"Absolutely not," Bev said. "Now you get on to bed. You've got livestock to judge in the morning."

CHAPTER SEVENTEEN

The next morning, Bev woke with the sun and Biscuit in his usual spot between her calves. She couldn't believe how…well, how content she was to have him back at the inn. Even with all his mischief, there was something about him that made it somewhat worth it.

That theory was tested when she moved, and Biscuit lifted his head to growl at her.

"Hey," Bev said. "Cut that out."

He stopped, licking his chops as if there was something distasteful in his mouth. Then he lowered his head back down and stared at her with wide, remorseful eyes.

"That's better," Bev said, sitting up and rubbing her face. It was still dark outside, and she had a mountain of chores—not the least of which was doing last night's dishes. But at least she didn't have to wander around town looking for a pig. And with any luck, today's livestock showing would go off without a hitch and it would be a nice, quiet day.

"Do we get those anymore?" Bev asked Biscuit.

He rolled over and went back to sleep.

Bev tossed the covers off and went first to her wash basin, then to her drawers to find a clean shirt. She was getting low—another thing to add to her growing list of chores for the day— but as she yanked one from the nearly-empty space, her gaze caught that amulet piece again.

She held it for a moment, rubbing her fingers on the jagged edges.

"Hey, Biscuit." She turned to the dog. "What do you think of this?"

He opened an eye then rolled over and fell asleep.

She walked to the bed and put it right under his nose. His snout twitched for a moment, but he made no moves.

"So nothing. It's not magical at all?"

A low exhale was the only response.

"Well, what about this?" Bev walked to the window and plucked the dried rosemary from the window. Biscuit lifted his head as she sat on the bed and gently sniffed the plant. But he made no move to eat it or go for it, lying back down and falling asleep. "Nothing, eh?"

Either one of two things were true: Biscuit was a very sensitive dog and *not* a laelaps, or the things Bev had been convinced were magical actually weren't. More likely the latter than the former, based on all the other evidence.

"Well, I suppose this amulet is a mystery for another day," she said, tossing the fragment back into her drawer and hanging the rosemary in her window again. "At least you aren't trying to eat it."

The other rosemary she was attempting to propagate seemed wilted and sad in the window. Bev rotated the pot and three rosemary leaves fell off. It certainly didn't appear to be taking root.

"C'mon, buddy," she whispered. "We have a lot riding on you. Perk up, will you?"

She gave him a bit more water and another pat to the planter before straightening.

"Well, Biscuit. Time to get to work."

The kitchen mess was dealt with faster than Bev had anticipated, and she even had time to get the bread proofing before heading out to the front hall to greet her guests in the morning. Allen arrived with his customary basket, and Biscuit was all too willing to snatch an apple muffin from his giving hands.

"Are you feeding him enough?"

Bev took a muffin for herself, and cast a look at Biscuit, who'd put his front paws on her leg and was staring at her with his big, golden eyes. "Back off. This is mine."

To her surprise, the dog sat back down.

"Seems like he's listening well. What are you calling him?" Allen asked.

"Biscuit," Bev said. "Thought it was a good name."

"I—"

Biscuit growled as Claude made his appearance —though this time through the front door.

"Knock it off," Bev barked at the dog, who immediately wilted in shame. "Sorry, Claude. One day, he'll warm up to you, I bet."

"I wouldn't count on it," Claude said with an understanding smile.

"You're up early."

"Just wanted to let everyone else know the pig had been found," he said. "I couldn't stomach the idea of townsfolk wandering the plains needlessly."

"Very nice of you," Bev said. "Come have a muffin."

As he approached, Biscuit growled again. "Biscuit, hush."

"Wow, he doesn't like you, does he?" Allen said,

giving the judge a once-over. "I don't think we've met. I'm Allen Mackey, from the bakery next door."

"Claude Bonding," he said, shaking the baker's hand. "Your goods are delicious. Almost magical, if I might add. Never had any so good."

Allen smiled and gave Bev a knowing look. "They used to say that about my mom's too, but I can promise you, not a drop of magic goes into my bowls and pans. Just flour, butter, sugar, and a lot of care."

"Whatever you're doing, keep it up," Claude said, taking a second muffin and stashing it in his pocket. "I'm going to run upstairs and change— need to look my best as we traipse around in the mud and muck for the showing this morning."

Biscuit watched Claude depart with a wary look then settled down to sleep by Bev's feet.

"He wasn't kidding. Dogs really don't like him," Allen said. "Well, I'd better be going. Gotta get an order of pastries to the tea shop and a couple more to Lazlo's house."

"Lazlo?" Bev frowned. "What's happening there?"

"Didn't ask. Not my business," Allen said. "But I think Mayor Twinsly was the one who personally put in the order yesterday. They must be having some kind of meeting." He shrugged. "I'll take the gold from whomever I can."

"Noted." She nodded to the muffins. "Thanks again for the delivery."

"Have a good one, Bev!"

~

Petula, for one, was glad to hear that the pig had been returned, because she was clearly *not* in the mood to have another competition bumped from its schedule. She also didn't have a complaint about Allen's muffins today, which in Bev's estimation was as good a compliment as any.

"Say, you aren't really going to write up those soldiers, are you?" Bev asked. "I mean, we found all the animals. Everything's going smoothly. No need to…well…"

"It's my *job* to ensure that Her Majesty's soldiers are adhering to every possible rule and protocol," she said, almost offended Bev would suggest otherwise. "And if they didn't want to be written up, they shouldn't have neglected their duties. It's not hard to stand and watch a field of creatures."

"No, it's not. Which is why it's so…odd to me that it happened how it did," Bev said. "We found goats and rabbits all over this town. Just seemed a bit more than—"

"However it happened," Petula interrupted, as if warning her not to talk about the *m* word, "as you said, it's all resolved now. So we should continue with our day."

And with that, she left.

"You know, Biscuit," Bev said quietly, looking down at the sleeping dog. "I think it might be time to test out that sniffer of yours. If only to save the careers of those innocent soldiers."

He sat up, eager to listen.

"I'm not sure how this works, exactly. But someone in town is using magic to mess up the festival." This was ridiculous, talking to a dog like he understood her. "Can you help me find whoever it is?"

He walked to the front door, and Bev, hopeful, followed.

～

At first, it seemed like Biscuit was wandering around town. He'd go to this corner and sniff, to that corner and pee, to this bush and sniff again. As they walked into the festival, the overwhelming scent of food was yet another distraction, and she had to pull him away from the turkey leg vendor—as she was quite sure he wasn't the man Bev was looking for.

"You know, this is starting to feel like a bad idea," Bev said. "Whatever kind of magical detector you are, you're easily swayed by food."

Eventually, he led Bev north, to the livestock showing pens. There was already a crowd of spectators leaning on the fence, watching the action in the center. Earl had constructed a low platform for the actual judging, where Petula, Claude, and Ida with her clipboard were inspecting a cow held by a farmer Bev didn't recognize.

A few steps from the platform, a queue of farmers stood ready with the rest of the bovines. Bev recognized a couple, including, surprisingly, Trent Scrawl. Bev would've thought he'd just entered the gourd competition, since he'd been so keen to show up Herman Monday all year long. But perhaps the farmer was a bit more multifaceted than she'd given him credit for.

Biscuit pressed his nose to the grass as he wove in and out of the spectators' feet. Bev watched carefully, ready to snatch him if he made a move to run into the judging pen, but so far, whatever he was searching for kept him out.

"Next, please," Petula called.

Another farmer guided their cow toward the platform, and the whole queue shuffled forward.

"I think that one has a chance," Hans Silver said to his husband Freddie. "She's got plenty of room from her hooks to her pins."

"Agreed. Very nice."

Biscuit walked right by Hendry, who was glaring daggers at her nemesis on the opposite side of the pen. The rest of the Middleburg delegation— including those who'd shown up to search for the missing livestock—were clumped near her as well.

"How's it going?" Bev asked Hendry, as Biscuit took a moment to stop and sniff a spot on the ground intensely.

"So far, so good. I hear you're the one who found the pig last night," Hendry said, not breaking her gaze from Twinsly. "That's good for us."

"Well, it's good for everyone," Bev said. "As we don't want a pig missing, right?"

"Yes, of course." She ran a nail along the line of her lips. "What's your dog doing? I thought you said he was gone."

"He's…uh…sniffing," Bev said, not wanting to get into an explanation.

Whatever Biscuit had been scenting, he seemed to have found it, because he lifted his head, nose twitching, then took off toward the holding pen for the rest of the animals. Bev quickly excused herself to follow him, hoping he wasn't smelling the animals' food.

Biscuit walked under the fence easily, marching steadfastly toward the gaggle of pigs in the center of the ring. Luckily, all attention seemed to be focused on the cow showing, and if anyone had anything to say, Bev could argue she was trying to get her dog.

Biscuit kept walking with his nose to the ground until he stopped in front of a pig. He sat and looked at Bev, expectantly.

"T... Biscuit, this is a pig."

He opened his mouth to smile at her.

She couldn't be sure, but it might've been the same pig she'd found the night before. It was certainly the same size and color, but there were others that seemed similar as well.

"This isn't very helpful," Bev said. "I'm looking for a *person*. Not the pig who escaped last night."

He stared at her as if she were the stupid one.

"Well, maybe there is something to this pig," Bev said. "I wonder who it belongs to—"

There was commotion from the other side of the ring, and for a moment, Bev feared someone had noticed her standing in the pen of pigs. But no, the crowd seemed interested in something in the judging arena.

Two men were out-and-out *brawling*.

She caught Trent Scrawl's face and knew immediately who the other fighter was. Herman Monday.

"Goodness gracious," Bev said. "Let's see what's gotten into them this time."

Bev jogged over, hopping the fence to the judging pen and hurrying the rest of the way. Petula and Claude were calling on the two to stop fighting, Hendry was trying to break in, and Twinsly was watching with a smirk on her face.

"What in the world's going on?" Bev asked.

"No clue," Hendry said. "We were standing here when Herman came out of nowhere and sucker punched Trent. Then they started..." She gestured to the two men wrestling on the ground. "This."

"Outrageous," Petula said. "Someone needs to intervene!"

Since no one spoke up, Bev sighed and said, "Claude, you grab Herman."

"Who's Herman?" he said, looking quite scared.

"I've got Herman," Freddie Silver said, coming up beside Bev. "One, two—"

He and Bev dove into the fray and grabbed whatever body part they could. Bev latched onto Trent's shoulder and pulled him backward while Freddie grabbed Herman by the neck and hoisted him away. The two were filthy and bloody, with torn shirts and pants as they stared murderously at each other.

"Now what in the green earth is going *on*?" Bev called, releasing Trent.

"No idea, Bev," Trent said, wiping his dripping nose. "This idiot came out of nowhere and started beating me up."

"Don't you know, you stupid codger!" Herman bellowed. "You! You! You ruined me!"

He took a step toward Trent again, but Freddie pulled him back.

"What did he do, Herman? Use your words,

please," Hendry said.

"*He destroyed my gourds!*"

A veil of silence descended on the crowd as everyone—including Trent—wore matching looks of shock.

"He did…what?" Petula said.

"This morning, I headed out to my patch to check on my babies, give 'em some water, get 'em ready for the competition. But when I got there… they were all…*smashed*." His eyes filled with tears. "Even the little ones I was saving to make pumpkin pies with. Destroyed."

Bev put her hand to her mouth. "No."

"I been growing them all season. Tenderly, lovingly, giving them all my attention," he said, wiping his eyes as he openly wept. "And this… this…this piece of dirt decided his weren't up to snuff and stomped out the competition!"

"You're a dirty liar!" Trent barked. "Why would I need to destroy yours when mine were bigger?"

"Were they?" Hendry asked.

"Well, obviously, I don't know for sure, but I think they were," Trent said, backpedaling. "But I may hate you with every fiber of my being, but I'd never stoop so low. I want to beat you fair and square." He paused, his voice cracking. "Are you sure? Every one?"

Herman began to sob. "All of 'em."

Bev blinked. Was Trent crying, too?

"You're absolutely sure?" Trent asked, stepping forward with tears leaking down his face. "Not one left?"

Herman shook his head. "Hard to say, of course, they were nothing b-but p-pieces…"

Then, to everyone's shock, the two men embraced and sobbed in each other's arms.

"Well, this is…a way to end a fight," Claude said, rubbing the back of his head. "But who destroyed his pumpkins?"

Hendry glared at Twinsly and opened her mouth, but Petula held up her hand. "I'm not going to entertain conspiracy theories. Mayor Hendry, this is *your* festival. I suggest you find the culprit."

Hendry's glare swept over to Bev, and she sighed. So much for a quiet day.

CHAPTER EIGHTEEN

Since no one else volunteered, Bev, Biscuit, Trent, and Herman trudged out toward Herman's farm to see the destruction. Trent and Herman were still arm in arm, softly crying to one another like long-lost brothers. Bev and Biscuit followed, Bev shaking her head and hoping this newfound peace would endure beyond the week.

When they reached the farm, Bev wasn't really prepared for the destruction—and by Trent's mournful howl, neither was he. There was nothing but seeds, innards, and pieces of the hull scattered around the trampled pumpkin vines. In fact, it almost looked like...

"Were any animals found here last night?" Bev asked Herman.

"I—*sniff*—don't know what you mean?"

"Last night, all the livestock got loose. They were all over the place," Bev said. "I wonder if one of them was found in your pumpkin patch and did this."

It was a plausible solution, for sure. Bev could check with Ida to see if any of the search parties had come this way. And it would at least be an explanation that didn't immediately bring forth more questions, more unclear motives, more hidden suspects.

"You didn't see anyone in your patch last night, right?" Bev asked. Herman nodded. "When did you last see your pumpkins, and when did you check them this morning?"

"Oh, um..." He put his hand to his forehead. "They were good this morning around five when I woke up to water them. But seven...by seven they'd been smashed."

Bev scowled. So much for the errant livestock theory.

"And you didn't see anyone out this way?" she pressed, running her fingers over the trampled vines.

"I can't..." He shook his head. "I can't bear to look at it."

"Come on, Hermy, let's get you back home and

make you a cuppa."

Trent half-carried his former nemesis back toward his house, leaving Bev and Biscuit to stare at the wreckage and do their own investigations. Bev knelt and ran her fingers along the destroyed pumpkins, looking for a foot- or hoofprint, but she couldn't discern much from the mess. Even though all the livestock had been put back in their pen, it still *looked* like one of them had been out here.

"C'mon, Biscuit," Bev said. "Let's put that sniffer to the test again."

She turned to the dog, finding him chewing on one of the pumpkin rinds.

"Oh, let's not add insult to injury," she said. "C'mon. Let's see what else we can find."

Bev wanted to check every possible theory before she left the farm, so she walked out to the road in search of prints or any other clues. As she was crawling in the brush, footsteps approached, followed by a horrified gasp.

"Oh, my..." Alice Estrich stood behind her. "I'd heard there was a brawl, but I didn't expect... Goodness gracious. Where's Herman?"

"Getting a cup of tea with Trent," Bev said, coming to her feet and wiping her knees. "They seem to have...uh...made up, I guess?"

"Miracles do happen, I suppose." She smiled. "Anything I can do to help?"

"Yeah, wondering—did you happen to see any of those missing livestock from last night out this way?" The timing didn't match up, but it didn't hurt to ask anyway.

"I saw the search parties, but I don't think they found anything," Alice said. "Didn't really speak to them, though, so don't quote me on that."

"I won't, but I appreciate the insight," Bev said. "I mean, this looks like it was trampled by a large animal. But also..." She glanced at Alice. "There's that whole magical river thing that's out this way, too."

"Oh, pish-posh." Alice stepped back, waving her hands. "Don't be saying that too loud or you'll be running afoul of the queen's folks who're in town." She chuckled. "If I didn't know any better, Bev, I'd say you were obsessed with magic."

"No, can't say I am," Bev replied. "I'm sure Herman would appreciate a check-in from his neighbor later on today. He's pretty heartbroken."

"I'll do that. Maybe bring him a pie..." She paused, making a face. "Just perhaps not a pumpkin one." She glanced at the ground. "Your dog seems to be...enjoying the remnants, doesn't he?"

Bev spun around and found Biscuit on his belly gnawing on a large piece of pumpkin held between his front paws.

"What did I say?" Bev bellowed to him. "Quit

eating the evidence, B!"

The dog dropped the pumpkin and sprinted away, this time under the fence and down the street.

"Drat," Bev said. "Guess I'd better follow him before he gets into more trouble. See you around, Alice."

Biscuit kept moving, slowing down to sniff bushes and lift his leg then speeding up when Bev got too close. She was once again perplexed by his behavior, as he was heading southeast, away from town. But when the familiar forest thicket appeared up ahead, she stopped and glanced at the sky.

"This stupid place again?" Bev sighed.

For the umpteenth time, she forced her way through the thicket and into the clearing. When she got there, Biscuit had something in his mouth. A piece of pumpkin.

"You didn't bring this here, right?" Bev said. No, the dog had dropped what he'd been chewing. And this was a huge piece, nearly the size of Biscuit's head.

So what in the world was a piece of Trent's pumpkin doing in this thicket...that seemed to be the repository for magic-laced objects?

Alice said Bev was obsessed with magic, but *magic* seemed to be the common thread between most of the mishaps. The bauble in the pie, Merv's magic blanket. Even though Biscuit hadn't been interested in Bev's rosemary, she could plausibly say there was something magical in there, too. The pig, too, was perhaps not as ordinary as it seemed. Now Herman's pumpkins, which had been grown in a magical river, had been destroyed.

"Is someone looking for magic?" Bev muttered. "Or am I seeing things I want to see?"

She took another tack, looking at the events from Hendry's perspective. Bev's rosemary and garden could've prevented her from being in the competition, leaving Stanton Bucko as the clear winner (that was, if Bev wanted to believe that her bread was that good). Next, the pie disaster—but that was when things fell apart.

If Hendry was right, and it was Middleburg, they wouldn't have toppled over a table with their own pies. There were Middleburg pie-makers who'd used late summer fruit and had to drop out of the competition.

Merv's blanket aside, there'd been Middleburg livestock missing, too. And although it could've been another debacle to mar the reputation of the Pigsend Harvest Festival, Bev couldn't see how any farmer from Middleburg would be fine with allowing their precious animals to wander off—even if it did mean moving the festival to their town.

No, as much as Hendry wanted it to be, Bev

couldn't see a clear motive for Middleburg. Which left her with her only other option: that someone was on the hunt for someone or something magical. Just like Karolina and her team had been.

"Biscuit, do you see anything?" she asked. "Well, smell anything, I should say."

She wasn't sure *what* exactly she was looking for —only that it seemed all the things that were "magic" had been found in this thicket. Biscuit, of course, kept finding more pumpkin pieces—and there were, in fact, several—but Bev walked around the clearing slowly, looking for anything that seemed amiss. She found a small thread of purple yarn from Merv's quilt in the brambles, more remnants from her garden swept off to the side, and not much else.

Then, Biscuit seemed to scent something, circling the clearing for a moment before diving into the brush. When he emerged, he had something that looked like a collar in his mouth.

"What's this?" Bev said, inspecting it closer. It was far too big to go around Biscuit's neck, so it wasn't his. Made of leather, with…

Bev's eyes widened. It was engraved with the queen's signet. And as Bev examined it, she realized that while it might've been too big for Biscuit, it was *just* the right size to fit around that pig's neck.

She rose slowly, holding the collar in her hands. There were only three out-of-town people who belonged to the queen—Petula and her two soldiers.

"Hm."

Bev chewed on this new thought as she walked back to the inn, Biscuit trotting alongside her.

Ridge had been on watch when the livestock had gotten loose. He'd been the one out searching, too, and had taken the errant pig back to the pen.

Or had he?

Had Ridge, instead of taking the pig back to the pen, taken it to Herman's house in search of... something, and trampled his pumpkins for some reason unknown?

She considered each incident from the festival and tried to remember if she'd seen Ridge there. But he'd been missing from the table incident, and the town hall had been empty when Merv's blanket had gone missing. But there was someone who'd been at each incident and who very obviously worked for the queen.

Petula.

It made zero sense. Why would a member of the queen's official judging corps want to ruin the festival?

Maybe the moving-to-Middleburg angle isn't so crazy after all.

Bev had never been so eager to serve a meal before. As she walked out with her platter of meat and potatoes, she scanned the room for Petula and —she hoped—her two soldiers, but only the latter seemed to be in attendance. Petula would come back eventually, so Bev would catch her then. It would be difficult to ask questions without arousing suspicion, but Bev had a few in mind.

Biscuit, for once, was behaving very well, sleeping on the floor behind the front desk. But he'd also had his fill of lamb and potato skins, so perhaps he was overfull and sleepy.

As dinner got underway and the conversations grew louder, Bev found herself watching the two soldiers intensely. They seemed to be chastened, eating with their heads down and not talking with anyone else in the room. Was it an act or were they actually concerned for their jobs?

Eventually, Ridge must've noticed her watching because he wandered over. "Hey, Bev."

"How are you enjoying the meal?"

"Everyone was right. This is the best place in town to get dinner." He offered a bashful smile, and Bev almost bought it. "Look, I just...I wanted to thank you again for finding that pig last night. I really felt awful about everything, and at least now, Ms. Banks may not be so harsh in her write-up."

Bev forced an understanding smile. "Glad to help. Say... Out of curiosity, can you tell me exactly what happened? It seems so...far-fetched to me."

"Well, Marcelano and I were standing on the southern end of the holding pen," he said. "The animals were wandering around, but some of them were settling in to sleep. So when they *all* got quiet, we kind of thought they'd gone to sleep."

"And you said they all got quiet at once, right? Like they disappeared together?"

He nodded.

"That pig that I brought back," Bev said. "Do you know who he belongs to?"

"No. Didn't ask. Just glad to have him back where he belonged. You can be sure that Marcelano and I didn't sleep a wink last night. In fact..." He yawned. "I'm glad there's nothing to watch tonight because I'm exhausted."

"I bet. I wish I had a room for you," Bev said. "Are you guys still staying in Middleburg or—"

"No, Mayor Twinsly was able to shuffle some of her people around and we're staying with Lazlo Murtagh." He smiled. "We're grateful, too. It's not a long ride back to Middleburg, but I'm glad I don't have to do it tonight."

"Uh-huh," Bev said. Another Middleburg connection. "Did Petula arrange that, by chance?"

"I'm not sure," he said. "Why?"

"Just trying to figure out whose side she's on," Bev said. "Seems like she's a little chummy with the Middleburg mayor. You know, Mayor Hendry and

Twinsly keep accusing each other of sabotage."

He chuckled. "Just ridiculous, you know? These things happen sometimes. There was a festival in Hammerstown that had a bunch of mishaps, too. They managed to keep their festival, but..." He leaned in closer. "If you ask me, I think the judge got a nice sum of money for keeping his mouth shut about it."

"Well, I'll have to tell Hendry to adjust her strategy," Bev said with a chuckle.

"I wouldn't. Petula Banks takes her job *very* seriously," Ridge said. "If she even gets the faintest whiff of scandal, she'll pull out her rule book, and all heck'll break loose."

"Do you always travel with her?" Bev asked.

"Oh, no. We all rotate around. This is my first time working with Petula, but I've heard things from my fellow soldiers. And every one of them has proven true." His eyes dimmed a little. "Which is why I'm grateful you at least found the pig. No telling what she'd do to us if we hadn't."

Bev actually felt bad for him. "Well, I hope you guys get some good rest tonight."

"I sure will after this delicious meal. Thank you again."

Middleburg was now back in the mix, muddying the waters. Bev had never been so unsure about anything in her life. Just when she seemed to have a clear answer…

The front door opened, and Ida came rushing in, her eyes wide with fear. "Bev! Bev, come quick."

"Oh, good green earth, what now?" Bev groaned. "More pumpkins smashed?"

"No, nothing about…" She beckoned Bev to follow her into the kitchen.

"What is it?" Bev said, closing the door behind her. "What's happened?"

Ida ran a hand over her hair, causing a couple curls to come loose from her tight bun. "Petula said she'd seen enough. She's ready to *officially* recommend the Harvest Festival be moved to Middleburg."

Bev put her hand to her chest. "Goodness, Ida. You came in here like someone had died."

"Bev, this is *serious*," Ida said. "She said she was ready to cancel it *today*. No more contests, no more festival. Done." She shook her head, pacing the room. "Obviously, Hendry and I tried to convince her that was a bad idea, that we were *looking* for the culprits, and Petula asked what we had and so…"

"Ida, what did you do?" Bev said, leaning in closer.

She winced as she lifted her gaze to meet Bev's. "I called for a town meeting. And asked for you, by name, to give your testimony."

Chapter Nineteen

In Pigsend, there were only a few tried-and-true rules, but one of the most important: when a citizen called for a town meeting, a town meeting *would* be held. As much as Bev didn't want to spend all night in the crowded meeting space, it was nothing compared to the dread of facing the town without anything to say.

Petula was currently her prime suspect in the festival mishap. But Bev also had to present evidence to her that she was guilty. Or risk having the entire festival cancelled for the year and moved to Middleburg.

Although it would have made for compelling

evidence, Bev didn't bring the collar. It would raise too many questions that Bev didn't have the answers to yet. It was entirely possible there was an innocuous reason for it being in the thicket. Or it was possible Bev was on the cusp of unraveling some kind of major conspiracy akin to the magical river and sinkholes.

Either way, she wasn't ready to show all her cards.

When she arrived at the meeting space in the town hall, it was *packed*. These meetings were usually well-attended, but with the addition of all the out-of-town folks, there was barely room to stand, let alone sit. Bev had to squeeze through the front door and a thick mass of people to get to the center walkway. There wasn't a place to sit on the benches, so she stood next to Earl Dollman and his friend Jane Medlam, the mason, and waited for the "festivities" to begin.

At seven on the nose, Hendry rose and held up her hands. The room immediately went silent.

"Good evening, citizens of Pigsend and honored guests," she said. "We're here because Ms. Ida Witzel has requested a town hall to discuss the matter of the Harvest Festival and the mishaps that keep occurring. We will ask a few individuals questions first then open the floor to anyone in the room who wishes to provide some insight into who or what might be causing the problems." She paused, clearing her throat. "Bev? Are you here?"

Bev sighed. Might as well get it over with.

She walked to the front of the room, hating that, yet again, she was the center of attention at one of these. Though she could count her blessings that she wasn't actually *sitting* at the front, which was where Ida, Hendry, and Petula were.

"Well, Bev," Ida said with more than a little trepidation, "what have you been able to uncover?"

"It's hard to find a common thread," Bev said, raising her voice so it would echo in the room. "Obviously, this started when a loaf of my bread went missing then my garden was destroyed." She paused, glancing at Petula. "Still haven't been able to figure that one out. Then, of course, the pies being overturned and, perhaps relatedly, Felicia's pie-making materials vanishing." Bev turned around to spot Felicia in the front row. "They're still missing, right?"

"They are," she said with a curt nod. "And I still think *you* did it."

"Anyway." Bev cleared her throat. "Merv's blanket is another curiosity, as is the livestock getting set free. I can't find a motive or a suspect that fits every single incident."

"Is that *so*?" Hendry asked. "What about Herman's pumpkins?"

vals

Bev hesitated, again debating if she should bring up the pig's collar and the thicket. "It's clear someone destroyed them sometime between the hours of five and seven this morning. I'd hoped, perhaps, it was one of the escaped livestock, but they were…well, my assumption was they were back in their pen this morning."

"They were," Ridge spoke up. "We made sure they were all accounted for."

Bev hid a small twitch. *So you say.* "I wish I had more to tell you. But as of right now, I'm stumped."

"But you *are* still investigating, right?" Ida said, her dark eyes dancing over to Petula. "Right?"

"Yes," Bev said. "I'll keep looking until I have an answer."

"Thank you," Ida said.

Hendry called on Petula's soldiers to give their testimony, and they told more or less the same story that Bev had heard from them. Next, Hendry called on Felicia and those who'd been in the room during the overturning. No one was able to definitively say who had tipped the table, though Felicia was sure to remind everyone Bev had been in the room.

"I was actually in Mayor Hendry's office," Bev replied, lightly.

"Well. She stole my pie-making supplies," Felicia said with a huff.

"Allegedly," Hendry said, dismissing her.

23

Next, she called on Rustin, who had nothing much of value to offer about when Merv's blanket had been destroyed—except, of course, to say that Petula and Claude were the last in the room before it had gone sideways.

Bev watched Petula's face closely, but the judge didn't display any sort of guilt.

"This concludes our individual questions," Hendry said. "Now, I'd like to open the floor to anyone who might have any evidence to offer or any other information that might lead to the culprit."

Surprisingly, the citizens of Pigsend didn't seem to have much to say on the matter. Not even Eldred Nest, who liked to spin wild conspiracy theories. Herman and Trent weren't even in the room, and they usually spent at least fifteen minutes apiece griping at each other.

"No one?" Hendry said, sounding disappointed. "No one has anything to add?"

"I do."

Ida's whole body went stick straight as her wife's voice rang out. Vellora rose from a spot in the middle of the room and slowly made her way to the front. Ida's paled, and her knuckles went white as her wife cleared her throat.

"I would like to say that, as a citizen of Pigsend, I wouldn't shed a single tear if we were to cancel this festival *right now* and have it never darken our door again."

Ida's cheeks grew dark as her gaze narrowed.

"Is that so?" Petula said. "You're the other butcher, are you not?"

"I am, ma'am," Vellora said, not making eye contact with her wife. "And I welcome anyone else who wants to agree with me to join me up here."

Bev was surprised—three or four people, including Alice Estrich, Etheldra Daws, and Sonny Gray stood to voice their agreement. Each one earned a death glare from Hendry, but Ida seemed to have checked out of the conversation.

"Does anyone else have anything to add related to the *topic* of this town meeting?" Hendry asked, her words laced with poison. "Anyone at all?"

No one said a word.

"Very well. I will take these facts into consideration," Petula said. "Consider the festival allowed to continue *as long as* there are no more screw-ups. And the final verdict on the location of the Middle-Southwestern Regional Agricultural Festival will be determined in a few days."

~

It was one of the shorter town halls in recent memory, and for that, Bev was grateful. Biscuit was waiting in the kitchen when she returned home and seemed to have kept himself out of trouble. He followed her around the kitchen as she started scrubbing plates and platters and prepping the kitchen for another round of baking in the morning.

She was about finished with everything when there was a soft knock on the door—so quiet that Bev almost didn't hear it. In fact, it wasn't until Biscuit walked to the door and sniffed that she went to open it.

Ida was on the other side, her eyes red-rimmed and her cheeks streaked with tears. "C-can I come in?"

"Oh, Ida, sure," Bev said, stepping back to allow her entry. "What's going on?"

"Oh, Vellora and I had a big fight. Perhaps the worst we've ever had." She wiped her eyes as she stood near the table. "I couldn't believe her standing up and saying that in the town hall. Like I haven't been killing myself for this festival. What happened to supporting each other, huh?"

"These things happen," Bev said gently. "Do you want a cup of tea? We can sit and talk about it."

"Got any beer left?"

"Plenty," Bev said with a smile.

Bev put the kettle on for herself then poured a pint for Ida, and they settled in at one of the empty tables in the front room. Ida took a swig from the tankard and put it down on the table, watching the suds for a while. The kettle whistled, and Bev returned to the kitchen to make herself a cup. When she came back, Ida was in the same position, a few more tears on her cheeks.

"I hate to see you so upset," Bev said softly. "Is there anything I can do?"

"Knock some sense into my wife," Ida said with a sardonic chuckle. "I don't know why she's so mad about the festival."

Bev *really* didn't want to get involved in their fight—a marriage was between two people and no one else—but she wanted to speak up on Vellora's behalf.

"You know, you've been awfully busy with the festival," Bev began softly. "I think Vellora's feeling the strain of doing all the work by herself. I know I've tripled my daily order. I understand the festival is important, but maybe…maybe she feels like you abandoned her, not the other way around."

Ida wiped her eyes. "Then she should've said something."

"I think she did. At least, she did to me." Bev took a hesitant sip of her tea. "Maybe you didn't hear her?"

Ida jutted out her lip. "Even if I did, we make more money during the week of festival than we do in a month. Moving it would be a huge blow to our income. And it seems like… She shouldn't have stood up and said that."

"No arguments there," Bev said, feeling like she

needed to assuage some of Ida's hurt. "I don't think it was the right move at all."

Ida sighed. "Maybe we could've… I don't know. Hired someone for the week of the festival to help out."

"Or you could've handed off the festival committee chairmanship to someone else," Bev offered.

"Nobody ever wants to take it," Ida said. "Precisely *because* it's so much work." She shook her head. "And to be honest, I like being involved. I like watching all the contests and competitions up close. I like to see this little town shine. I wish my wife would see how important this is to me."

"I know she knows," Bev said. "But there has to be a balance. You can't disappear during the busiest week of the year, and she can't be mad at you for doing what you love, right? I don't know how you square that circle." She took another sip of her tea. "Perhaps why I never married."

"Never?" Ida asked. "Not even…before you came to town?"

"Well, if I had a spouse, I'd hope they would've come looking for me," Bev said with a chuckle. "Who knows, maybe in a few months, some stranger will show up in town claiming to be married to me."

"One can dream," Ida said. "But you know, if

that doesn't happen, I think you're pretty happy here. And that's all one really wants for their friends."

"Agreed." Bev covered her hand and squeezed. "I know that emotions are high, but you and Vellora are the best team in town. I know you'll figure a way through this rough patch and be stronger than ever."

"Stronger…" Ida made another noise. "That's another thing she brought up tonight. She wants me to look into this…well, my weird ability to…"

"Your magical strength?" Bev said with a knowing look.

"Let's not call it that until we know what it is," Ida said, her eyes darkening.

Bev couldn't call it anything else. The slight woman could lift weights three times her size, and her strength evaporated when she touched iron. If that wasn't a magical ability…

"Nobody else in my family had anything of the sort," Ida said. "At least, nothing that my folks told me about. Vellora wants me to look into my family tree, visit the library, look through the town records. But I just…" She shook her head. "I'm afraid of what I might find." She paused, taking a shaky breath. "I thought maybe if I threw myself into the festival, the idea might blow over, and we could just go on. But I don't like the idea of knowing what I might have. I'd feel like I was carrying a target on my back."

"Ida, dear…" Bev began slowly. "You have very *obvious* strength. I think you have a target on your back whether you know what you are or not. But if you know, at least you'll be more prepared to answer."

"I think that's why Vellora wants me to investigate," Ida said. "She's so scared something will happen to me."

Bev smiled. "She's crazy about you. That much is true. You know—"

Biscuit barked in the kitchen, and Bev rose to see what the commotion was about. When she opened the door, Vellora was on the other side, looking much smaller than her large frame usually suggested.

"Is…um…Ida here?" she asked, not meeting Bev's gaze.

"In the dining room," Bev said, opening the door. "I'll give you two some privacy."

~

Bev returned to cleaning the kitchen, keeping an eye on the time. She didn't hear raised voices from the other room, so she hoped their conversation was at least civil, if not productive. She found herself sweeping toward the front door and listening but couldn't hear much. Finally, after half an hour, she cracked open the door.

The two women were sitting with their hands clasped together at the table. Ida had tears in her eyes but a soft smile on her face. Vellora caught Bev's gaze and chuckled. "You can come in now."

"Everything good?" Bev asked.

Ida nodded. "I think so."

"Good." Bev opened the door wider, and she and Biscuit joined the two butchers in the dining room. "Can't have Pigsend's best butchers at odds with one another."

"We're the only butchers," Vellora replied.

"Exactly. The whole economy would collapse."

Biscuit propped his paws up on Ida's leg and rested his head there. She cooed as she petted him. "You know, I think this little dog is starting to grow on me."

"He does that," Bev said. "But I'm pretty sure he's not a dog."

She explained the concept of a laelaps, and how Biscuit seemed to fit all the criteria. Ida scratched his ears, and he grunted as he leaned into her hand, earning another soft sigh from her.

"We're not getting a dog, Ida," Vellora said.

"I'll come over and play with Biscuit," she replied. "Assuming you're keeping him, Bev?"

"Unless his owner shows up," she said.

"Interesting what you said about him finding magical items," Ida said. "So you really don't have any theories, Bev?"

"I have one prime suspect," Bev said slowly, glancing up the stairs to make sure no one was listening. "And I'm afraid she was sitting next to you at the town meeting."

"Hendry?" Vellora said, making a face.

"Petula?" Ida gasped after a moment. "You can't be serious. Why in the world would she be involved?"

"I don't know," Bev said. "I can't pin down a motive. I do know that she's been present for every mishap."

"By that logic, you could blame me or Claude, too," Ida said. "Petula's not... I don't think she's behind this."

Bev told her about finding the pig in the thicket, then finding a pig-sized collar with the queen's signet afterward. "This may be a stretch, but my gut says that pig isn't really a pig, and maybe he's a magical sniffer like Biscuit. And *his* familiar is our real culprit."

"You could blame those soldiers," Vellora said. "They work for the queen, too."

"They're on my list, too, for sure," Bev said. "But I can't place them at half of the mishaps. It's hard to accuse someone of being responsible for something they weren't present for."

"I'll keep an eye on Petula tomorrow," Ida said

with a firm nod. "That is...um... Vellora, do you need me to stay behind and help at the store?"

Vellora reached across the table to take her wife's hand. "You help Bev. I can manage another couple of days."

Ida smiled. "How about you take next week off, and I'll manage the shop solo?"

Vellora leaned across the table to kiss her wife sweetly. "Deal."

Chapter Twenty

There was an air of trepidation in the village when Bev awoke the next morning. Even Biscuit seemed on edge as he watched her do her morning chores. Today was the gourd competition, typically the most well-attended event of the entire festival. And it was Pigsend's last chance to prove to Petula that they could and *should* keep this festival—and perhaps Bev's last chance to find the saboteur.

Bev, Ida, and Vellora had come up with a plan for the contest to keep the list of people inside the town hall small. And, in the morning, when Petula came down for her morning pastry, Ida would be on hand to offer the plan.

"It's so *early*," Ida yawned, leaning on Bev's counter. "Do you really get up this early every morning?"

"Mm," Bev said. "Do you want another cuppa?"

"Perhaps not. I'm jittery enough as it is." She nodded at Biscuit, who was splayed out in front of the fire, snoring loudly. "At least one of us gets to sleep."

"He's good at that," Bev said. "Have another muffin. Small consolation for getting up so early."

"I've had three," Ida said. Then, after a breath, she grinned devilishly. "Okay, maybe one more." She dove into it, letting out a moan of happiness. "Allen's outdone himself again. Pumpkin on the gourd contest day?"

"He's getting a little cheeky with his baking," Bev said with a smile. "You do love to see it."

Upstairs, a door opened, and Ida straightened, turning to watch the staircase as Petula made her way down.

"Oh, good morning, Ms. Witzel," Petula said, stopping short on the upper stair. "What brings you over here so early? Surely, it can't be the sub-par baked goods."

Ida forced a smile as she put down the half-eaten muffins. "Well, I wanted to follow up on yesterday's town meeting. I think we have a good plan that will keep the chaos to a minimum. It's not ideal, of course, but—"

"Well? I don't have all morning."

"I think, instead of the usual audience, we limit the gourd competition attendance to contestants and judges. If something goes wrong, we'll have a shortlist of people to question. But hopefully, nothing will, and we can continue with the festival."

Petula stared at her, seeming to digest this information as well as the pumpkin muffin. "It's not standard, for sure. But there's nothing in the rule book about restricting access, I suppose."

"I agree it's not ideal," Ida said. "But if it's a choice between the festival closing early or allowing our farmers to compete, I think there would be unanimous consent to the latter."

"Very well. I trust you'll inform the soldiers and handle the security." Petula put the rest of the muffin in the small bin near the front desk. "And in the meantime, I'm off in search of a decent breakfast pastry."

~

"I still think she's up to something," Bev said as she helped Ida set up the tables in the town hall. Ida, of course, was doing all the heavy lifting, and Bev was simply adding the tablecloths and helping write up the numbers for each entry. "She left in a hurry."

"It's certainly fishy," Ida agreed. "She did agree

to the plan, though. So perhaps a mark in her favor." She sighed as she easily moved the last table into position. "My sincere hope is that *nothing* goes wrong today or tomorrow, and we can close out this festival as a half-win."

"It's only the gourd contest today, right?" Bev asked. "Nothing else?"

"Just the vendors outside," Ida said. "So…well, I don't want to say nothing will go wrong, but it's hard to see how anything can."

Never say never, Bev thought to herself, but didn't want to voice it.

"Uh, good morning, ladies!" Sheriff Rustin walked into the hall, his voice booming. "I was told you were looking for me, Ida?"

Ida walked over to explain the new situation to him, and, although perplexed, the sheriff did as he was instructed. Farmers had already begun arriving to offload their entries. Pumpkins larger than wheelbarrows were carried in by any means necessary, sometimes requiring two or three different people. Trent Scrawl's pumpkin was easily the largest, but more surprising was that he and Herman carried it in together.

"I guess they've really buried the hatchet," Ida said, eyebrows raised.

"One can only hope," Bev replied with a chuckle.

"What do you mean, I can't come in?"

Mayor Twinsly's voice echoed from outside the hall, and Bev motioned to Ida that she'd handle it. Bev strode out to see Rustin looking uncomfortable as he stood in front of the door with his hands crossed.

"Ah, Mayor Twinsly," Bev said. "With all the… um…*mishaps*, we've decided to limit attendance to the contest entrants."

Twinsly snorted. "Surely, you can make an exception for the mayor of Middleburg."

"Sorry, no exceptions," Bev said, stepping out of the way to allow a farmer with a massive yellow squash to pass through. "We do hope you understand."

She made a face and stormed off, mumbling something about Hendry and her mismanaged festival.

"Boy, she's terrifying," Rustin said, rubbing the back of his neck.

"A bit," Bev said with a chuckle. "But nothing you can't handle, hm?"

There were more arguments, more people who wanted to be let in and couldn't, and some who outright threw a tantrum when their spouse was allowed inside and they weren't. Bev hated that they'd had to implement this security measure, and hated even more that she still didn't have any solid motive.

But her three top suspects arrived together, with Petula leading the way. Bev watched them for any signs of guilt, but Ridge waved to her nicely and Marcelano had a sheepish grin as he nodded to Rustin.

"Morning, Rustin," Marcelano said. "Bev."

Petula didn't seem to have time for niceties. "Is Mr. Bonding here yet?" she asked, her nose in the air.

"Not yet," Bev said. "At least, I haven't seen him."

Petula glanced at a pocket watch before tucking it away. "It's nearly time for the contest. Punctuality is important for judges. Something that Mr. Bonding's aunt seemed not to impress upon him."

She stepped inside after that, and Bev scanned the festival beyond for any sign of Claude. She and Ida had come straight here after Petula had agreed to the plan, so she hadn't had a chance to greet him this morning.

Finally, about a minute to ten, Claude came running up the street, his face red with exertion and his hair a mess, babbling his apologies about sleeping in until he realized that Bev and Rustin were all but blocking his path.

"Bev, what are you..." He straightened. "What's going on?"

"We've limited entry to judges and contestants to avoid…uh…another incident," she said. "So it's a small crowd in there today."

"And Petula went for it?" he asked with a raised brow.

"Supposedly, it's not against the rules," Bev said. "But she's mentioned your lateness already, so you might want to get in there."

"Oh goodness. Thank you!"

He dashed inside, and Bev followed, lingering near the door as she motioned to Ida. The butcher gave her a thumbs-up, and Bev poked her head out to Rustin.

"That's all the contestants," she said. "If you wouldn't mind staying here to keep an eye on things."

"I suppose." He sighed as he took a seat on the front step. "I really wanted to go shopping today."

"Won't be long, I promise," Bev said.

She ducked back inside and took a seat at the back of the hall. Ida was in the process of handing out numbers as Petula and Claude spoke in hushed tones in the corner.

"All right, I think we're ready," Ida said. "If I could ask all the farmers to vacate the room, please."

A roar of protest echoed from the attendees, none of whom wanted their most-prized possession out of sight. Ida was taken aback by the ferocity, and cleared her throat as Petula and Claude looked on.

"This is merely a precautionary measure," she said. "The only people in the room will be Ms. Banks, Mr. Bonding, and myself."

But her words were drowned out by the raucous arguments, and Ida seemed to admit defeat. "Fine, but you need to go sit on the first row of benches, at least. And please keep comments to yourself during the judging."

Slowly, with much trepidation, the farmers left their precious gourds on the table and sat on the benches near the front of the room.

"Um. Ms. Er... Bev." Ida was looking at her nervously. "Petula wanted me to remind you that... um...there will be no one else in this room except contestants and the judges. Which I think is code for—"

"Do you think you can keep an eye on things?" Bev asked. "What about Ridge and Marcelano?"

"We've been given the boot as well," Ridge said with a smile.

Bev didn't like the sound of that. "Maybe we can relieve Rustin and keep watch on the door. Ida, are you sure you can handle things in here?"

She nodded. "There's only going to be us three near the gourds. If something goes awry, there's no way I'll miss it."

~

Rustin was pleased to be relieved from guard duty, so Bev took his spot on the front step while the soldiers flanked her on either side.

"All this security for a little festival," Ridge said.

"Well, when you've got this much on the line," Bev replied with a shrug. "We really want this festival to continue. Brings in a lot of money." She sat back on her hands, hoping she sounded confused and not accusatory. "I can't imagine *anyone* would want to cause harm here."

"Oh, she might," Ridge said, nodding to Twinsly, who was lurking around one of the vendor booths. "She's been talking about how she wants this thing in her town."

"Yeah, she might," Bev said with a chuckle. "But why would she threaten her own townsfolk's wares?

"That's how they throw you off the scent!" Marcelano said with a small laugh. "Get you thinking they're innocent then cut your legs off!"

Bev and Ridge turned to stare at him as he coughed nervously.

"I read a lot of fiction," he said.

"Every time I think I have an answer, something else pops up that doesn't make sense," Bev said.

"Then maybe you don't have all the information?" Marcelano said. "Maybe someone's got an ulterior motive that you don't know about."

"You gotta quit reading so much," Ridge said.

Bev hated to admit it, but he had a point. There were large gaps in her understanding of things, and until she uncovered those, she'd be hopelessly lost.

"Bev, listen…do you think Marcelano and I could step over there and grab one of those delicious-smelling turkey legs?"

"We didn't get breakfast," Marcelano said with a frown.

"No, no, go on," Bev said.

They didn't go far, walking to the turkey-leg vendor nearby and purchasing one each. Then they stood off to the side as they joked and talked and devoured their meal. If they'd been looking to disappear, they probably could've suggested a different vendor, or even gone to eat somewhere else. But they stayed put.

As Bev sat there, a shadow passed over her face.

"Just a *shame* I can't be in there to support my farmers."

Mayor Twinsly was back, perhaps thinking Bev was easily overpowered with the soldiers gone.

"Do they need much support from their mayor?" Bev asked, keeping one eye on the soldiers. "They seem to have it handled."

"Well, it may come as a surprise to you here in Pigsend, but caring for one's citizens is a hallmark of a good mayor," she said. "Perhaps if you ever wised up and dumped Jo Hendry, you might be able to see that."

Bev made a face, unable to help herself. "Why do you and Hendry have such bad blood, anyway? I've never seen you together."

"Oh, I have no problem with her," Twinsly said with a forced laugh. "But she, bless her, has never forgiven me for moving out of Pigsend and becoming mayor of a larger town."

"You're from Pigsend?" Bev said with a start.

"Why, of course." Twinsly chuckled. "My maiden name is Murtagh. Lazlo and Wilda are my cousins."

Bev nodded slowly. "That...makes a lot of sense."

"I grew up with the Pigsend Harvest Festival," she said, almost a little wistfully. "It used to be so much nicer, you know. I was ecstatic when I heard that the queen's judging corps would be here, and they'd be able to move it to Middleburg."

"So you do want that, hm?" Bev asked. "Badly enough that you'd sabotage us?"

"Oh, dear Bev, I don't need to *do* anything. Clearly, Jo Hendry's capable of mismanaging the festival on her own." She chuckled. "But it's cute you want to blame me. I hear you're the local sleuth in town."

"Unwillingly."

"I—"

Whatever she was going to say was lost at the sound of a loud cry in the distance. Followed by another then another. Bev caught the attention of the two soldiers, and they dropped their turkey legs without another thought, running toward the sound of the commotion, with Bev hot on their tails.

Bev hadn't a clue what to expect now—it seemed everything that could've gone wrong *had*, but she was a woman constantly being surprised.

Chapter Twenty~One

"What in the..." Bev let out a breath. "Okay, this is..."

It was...the strangest sight Bev had ever seen. Roughly a quarter of the vendor tents had been flattened—trampled, almost. Tables, produce, gourds, more turkey legs were strewn about the space like a nasty storm had blown through. And standing on top of the mess were...

"How the heck did the livestock get out again?" Ridge said, his hand on his head.

"Who was supposed to be watching them?" Bev asked.

"Nobody," Marcelano said. "Most of the farmers

from Pigsend took theirs home yesterday. The only ones that were left were from Middleburg and places beyond."

Bev estimated no fewer than fifty cows, twenty goats, and a mess of other creatures walking around the space. It was…well, it didn't make *any* sense. There'd only been twenty cows in the pen to be judged in the first place. And if a number of them had gone back to their home pastures already…

"Did these come from somewhere else?" Bev asked, walking up to the first cow and checking for a tag or collar. This one had a marker that belonged to a Middleburg farmer. Another nearby had the same marker.

"I'm flummoxed," Ridge said.

A murmuring began behind Bev as the festivalgoers, drawn by the cries and loud sounds, made their way toward the northern part of the town square. Twinsly stood off to the side, her lips pursed in disbelief.

Bev couldn't help herself as she walked over. "Do you know anything about this?"

"Me? Why would I?"

"Because there are three times as many cows here as there are supposed to be—and the only ones left are from Middleburg," Bev said, her voice rising with frustration. "Quit playing dumb. What in the world is going on?"

"I wish I could tell you, *Bev*, but I had nothing to do with this," she said, her eyes flashing. "And I suggest you stop casting baseless accusations and start tending to your fellow citizens." She turned to walk away. "I'm going to get Petula."

Bev glared at her retreating back. Twinsly may not have been responsible, but she'd sure capitalize on it.

Nearby, Alice was shooing away a goat who'd been chomping down on her smashed potatoes and rutabagas.

"Oh, Alice," Bev said softly, kneeling to help gather what she could. "Are you all right? What in the world happened?"

"Well, I was sitting in my tent, vending, you know. It was a slow morning so far. Then I heard this loud rumbling and the sound of cows. I stepped out of my booth in time to see… It was like a *wall* of livestock coming into the space here."

Bev looked around again. It seemed there were fewer animals now than even a few moments before. "How many, do you think?"

"A hundred, at least," Alice replied. "Enough to send us all running to safety. When it stopped, we came back to…well, this." She gestured to the trampled space. "It's the strangest thing I've ever encountered."

"You say a hundred animals?" Bev shook her

head. "Any idea where they might've come from? Who all has livestock up toward the northern pasture?"

"Not many," Alice said with a shake of her head. "Most of those tending to livestock are farther south."

It makes no sense.

Bev couldn't get that refrain out of her head as she chewed on the situation. She wasn't sure what— if anything—she could've done differently. It wasn't as if she could be in ten places at once, watching every aspect of the town and hoping someone would show themselves. And if someone had magic…well, it was like Marcelano had said. It was hard to know the full picture of the situation when she was missing important details.

By now, Hendry had been alerted and was canvassing the vendors, making sure they were all right and finding out what they'd lost. Rustin, too, was in the mix, helping to move tents so vendors could retrieve items from beneath the wreckage.

"What d'ya reckon, Bev?" Rustin asked her.

"Honestly, I don't know," Bev said. "I'm stumped."

"What in the…"

True to her word, Twinsly had gone to retrieve Petula. She and Ida, along with the farmers who'd been in the judging contest, had walked into the chaotic scene. Ida's eyes were wide as she pressed her hand to her forehead, and Petula's lips were pressed into a tight line.

"Does anyone care to explain what happened?" Petula asked.

"If I had a good explanation for you, I'd give it," Bev said. "Best I can tell...a herd got loose and trampled the tents."

"Is anyone hurt?"

"No," Hendry said, her voice full of defeat. "How in the world was there a herd of livestock that got loose?"

"Seems like they moved on," Petula said. "I only count five cows and a goat."

Bev spun, shocked. That was the third number she'd heard in the past few minutes. So either Alice and the others had been seeing things or...

...or there was something magical afoot.

"Was there anything weird in the gourd competition?" Bev asked Ida as Petula started walking around to check each vendor.

"No. Not a thing. We were about to finish when Twinsly came barging in," Ida said. "What in the *world*, Bev?"

"I think someone's used magic," she replied. "Alice said there was a herd of a hundred cows that did the initial damage. I don't know about you, but I don't see a hundred cattle milling about right now, do you?"

Ida shook her head. "But *who*? And why would someone affiliated with the queen be casting spells like this? And for what purpose?"

"I haven't the foggiest," Bev said. "Wait…what's going on over there?"

Hendry had turned to Petula with a furious look on her face and had started arguing with her. Petula had her arms crossed and her nose up in the air, looking unfazed.

"…something foul is afoot, and this *isn't* Pigsend's fault," Hendry said as Bev and Ida ran over to them.

"Unfortunately, my decision is final," Petula said, adjusting her tunic.

"Please, Petula—" Hendry said. "Let us look into this, find whoever's responsible."

"It's clear that this town is not capable of putting on such a festival," Petula said. "You're lucky no one got hurt. Therefore," she straightened, "the Pigsend Harvest Festival is officially cancelled and will be moved to Middleburg next year. And that decision is now final."

A hush fell over the crowd as Hendry's hands fell helplessly to her sides. She put her hands over her face and sighed deeply. Ida released a sob but held herself together for the most part. Even Twinsly looked…well, she didn't look *happy*, so that was something.

"This isn't a decision I make lightly," Petula said quietly. "But after all I've witnessed, it seems we need to make a change. I'm sorry for having to be the bearer of bad news. Please begin the process of tearing down your tents and banners and clear the town as quickly as possible."

And with that, she turned and walked away.

"Not if I have anything to do with it," Hendry growled, balling her fists as she marched behind Petula.

"I suppose... I suppose we'd better start cleaning up," Ida said, her voice faint. "Let's start with the trampled tents. I'll...I'll get a wagon." She wandered off, her shoulders slouched and her feet shuffling.

"Well, I hope you're happy," Bev said to Twinsly. "You got what you wanted, after all."

Twinsly frowned, saying nothing as she followed Hendry and Petula.

The rest of those gathered moved as slowly as Ida, almost like zombies. The silver lining was that this was the penultimate day of the festival, so luckily, most of the vendors' wares had been sold. But the larger catastrophe was the Pigsend Festival would be no more—and that was what hung heavy in Bev's heart as she turned to walk back toward the inn.

Wearily, she walked through the front door, where Biscuit was waiting for her. He trotted over to greet her, sniffing and dropping his ears as if he knew she was upset about something.

"Tough day, boy," Bev said, scratching Biscuit under the ears. "Looks like we didn't save the Harvest Festival after all."

He didn't seem to know or care what was going on, except that Bev was sad, so he leaned against her, perhaps in an attempt to comfort her.

"You know, you aren't so bad to have around. Nice to have someone to talk to every once in a while. Even if you do want to eat me out of house and home." She chuckled as she scratched his rear.

He opened his mouth to smile then tilted his head as if to question her.

"Well, the long and short of it is this: Someone's out to sabotage the festival. I'm pretty sure it's Petula Banks, but I don't have any hard proof. Ida didn't see anything out of the ordinary today, and clearly...well, clearly someone wanted the Harvest Festival to go. Petula's cancelled all the other events, including the baking competition final. And the town should be emptying out tomorrow. It'll be sad, but..." She sighed. "Maybe it's for the best that the thing moves to Middleburg."

He nudged her again.

"Honestly, I'm more frustrated that I couldn't figure out *why* Petula wanted the thing to move? Why Middleburg? And why go through all the trouble to move it clandestinely? She's the member of the queen's official judging corps. She could move the festival by…saying so. It doesn't make any sense to me." She sighed. "Maybe Vellora's right. Maybe it was the soldiers." She paused. "No, they were *outside* the judging room the whole time—so was Mayor Twinsly." She shook her head. "It's a real stumper, that's for sure."

Biscuit took a few steps backward then put his nose to the ground and started walking.

"Thanks for listening," Bev said with a haphazard wave. "Do you need to go out back or—"

With a firm *swipe*, he pushed open the kitchen door and let himself out into the main hall.

"Biscuit?" Bev rose and followed him. "Where are you— *Hey!*"

That little butthead was halfway up the stairs, seeming to scent something.

Bev dashed behind him, grateful all the doors to the guest rooms were closed. But as she reached the landing, Biscuit practically pried one of them open to let himself in.

"*Biscuit!* Bad boy!" She scrambled after him, annoyed she'd have to go into a guest's room without their permission. It was an egregious breach of privacy. But Biscuit wasn't listening, and she needed to snatch him before he destroyed something.

She found him scratching and gnawing at the floor, and when she went to lift him, she found that the floorboard came up a bit with him. It was... loose.

"That's...new." Bev knelt to inspect it. One of the nails in the floor was missing, and the entire piece lifted easily. She wasn't trying to pry, but the well-worn satchel hidden between the floor joists caught her attention. With the pack exposed, Biscuit nosed the leather, trying to get under the flap and to the contents inside.

"Relax," Bev snapped. "I'm looking, I'm looking."

Carefully, she opened the satchel and uncovered a bevy of items that bore the queen's signet. This wasn't surprising—Petula worked for the queen. But the items inside weren't anything that a member of the official judging corps would have.

An iron knife was the most surprising, as was a pocket-sized book that seemed to contain the same magical creatures as in Bev's large tome. There was a small dowsing rod, about the size of Bev's palm. Bev had used such a thing when she'd hunted for the magical river, but seeing one so little...

Also in the bag was a diary of sorts.

Bev (no last name given)

Status: Unsure

Owner of the Weary Dragon Inn. Possible Magical, though exact race unclear. Shows no sign or inclination. Owns a laelaps. Rosemary in garden tested but results inconclusive.

Ida Witzel

Status: Magical

Co-owner of Witzel Butcher Shop. Possible dryad or nymph with extraordinary strength, though does not appear to hide powers. Wife is former Kingside soldier.

Jo Hendry

Status: Unsure

Mayor of Pigsend. Possible siren. ~~Appears unaware of powers.~~ Appears aware of powers and uses them to coerce townsfolk when *necessary, example was town meeting.*

Bev continued down the list, putting her hand to her mouth as her heart beat faster. Nearly everyone in town had been put on this list, and more than a few of them Petula seemed to think were magical. She again looked at her own name but was more drawn to Ida. So all Ida's fears about being targeted were coming true.

Yet, it didn't seem… If Petula knew all these people were magical, why wasn't she arresting them? Was she waiting for something?

Bev stopped reading and put all the things in the satchel, putting it back under the floorboard where she'd found it. She would take this information to Hendry and see…but what could be done? Unless Bev called another town meeting then forced Petula to come clean, as she'd done with Karolina and the others. But the information in this book was dangerous to everyone in town.

She rose, making sure everything was as she'd found it, and snapped her fingers to coax Biscuit from the room. He seemed hesitant at first, but followed, and she shut the door behind her, mind spinning.

What to do, what to…

She stopped as she hit the first step of the stairwell, turning slowly to look behind her.

Biscuit hadn't run into Petula's room.

He'd run into Claude's.

CHAPTER TWENTY~TWO

Bev returned to the room to grab the satchel then sprinted out of the inn, stopping only to call on Ida to join her. She didn't ask questions—and Vellora was right behind her. The trio, with Biscuit trailing behind happily, sprinted toward the town square in search of Petula—and Claude.

They found Petula near the town hall, fielding questions from angry farmers and vendors, not to mention Hendry and Twinsly, who seemed as angry, if not more, at the queen's judging corps member.

Petula turned when Bev came running up, her eyebrows rising. "What in the world...? What's going on?"

"Where is Claude?" Bev asked, breathless.

"Well, I don't know, I assume back at the inn packing up his things."

"No." Bev shook her head. "He's not. Where…" She narrowed her gaze at the town hall. "There. He's in there."

The group, now joined by the two mayors, who didn't ask questions, ran toward the town hall building. More joined them—Hans and Freddie Silver, Alice Estrich, even Etheldra Daws gathered in a large clump as Bev and the rest ran up the front steps.

But as Bev pushed on the front doors, they wouldn't budge.

"It's…locked," Bev said with a gasp. "Jo, do you have a key?"

"Not on me," she said. "Bev, what's going on?"

"I'll have an answer for you in a bit," Bev said, pulling at the door. "How long until you can—"

"Let me." Ida walked forward and with a yell, kicked open the doors. She turned sheepishly to Hendry. "We'll replace that."

"Never mind," Hendry said, pushing past her. "What are we… Oh my goodness."

The town hall room was a *mess*. The prized pumpkins that had been in the process of being judged were all in smashed pieces on the ground. The large pig Bev had found in the thicket was nosing through the remains, snorting loudly as he went.

And Claude stood with an uncharacteristically stoic look on his face, jotting down things in a diary not unlike the one Bev had in his satchel. He stared at the interruption, frozen for a moment as the wheels seemed to turn in his head. Then, he put the journal away and walked toward them.

"I'm so glad you guys made it. I... Well, I found this pig in here—"

"Give it up," Bev tossed his satchel on the ground in front of him. "I know you were behind it. All of it."

He stared at his satchel then narrowed his gaze. "I suppose there's no privacy at your inn, is there?"

"Well, my dog broke into your room," Bev said. "He's a bit intentional when he wants to be. But I think you knew that about him."

"I don't understand," Petula said. "What is the meaning of this? What is that satchel? What is—"

"Yes, Claude," Bev prompted. "Why don't you explain to us exactly who you really are and what you're doing here?"

He paused. "And why should I do that?"

Petula puffed out her chest, affronted. "Because as a member of the queen's official judging corps—"

"I hate to inform you of this, Ms. Banks, but I actually outrank you," he said with a smile. "My name is Renault Lank, and I'm a member of Her Majesty's Special Service."

The room went silent, as even Bev found herself without words. Of all the things she'd expected... sweet, gentle, affable Claude really being a hardened member of the queen's service certainly wasn't one of them.

Bev swallowed. "So you work with Karolina?"

"No, of course not." He chuckled. "She works in one branch, and I'm in a different, specialized unit." He paused, perhaps debating if he should say more. "My job is to search for powerful magical users. The kind that legends are made from. And the kind that...well, the kind that run afoul of Her Majesty's desires for this kingdom."

Bev's chest constricted. "And do what with them?"

"Her Majesty has a *vested* interest in making sure these individuals are brought to her court and given a thorough review."

A nervous hum rippled through the crowd behind Bev. Vellora clutched her wife's hand, Hendry had paled somewhat, and others who'd joined the fray seemed uncomfortable.

"So?" Bev asked, lifting her head. "Did you find anyone?"

"I suppose you read the journal," he scoffed. "And you'll be pleased to know that while there's a *great deal* of illegal magic happening around here, none of it rises to the level that I'm concerned with."

Bev tried not to look relieved, nor did she look at Ida, even though she desperately wanted to.

"There should be *no* magic *anywhere*," Petula said, stomping her foot. "And if you know of any, you need to report it to me straight away."

"As I said, Petula, I outrank you, so I don't report to you," Renault replied with a flippant tone.

"Why are you here, then?" Hendry asked. "And why are you ruining our festival?"

"A byproduct of my job, I assure you. I couldn't care less about your festival and where it happens to be." He paused, perhaps realizing he wasn't going to get out of this room without a satisfying explanation. "Very well. As I said, my job is to search out the most powerful magical users in the kingdom. Many of them have fled to remote parts of the kingdom where they believe the reach of the queen doesn't extend, such as quiet little towns like this." He cracked a smile. "But these sorts of festivals have a way of...bringing forth magical creatures and objects, you know? Given a chance to shine, they can't help themselves and tend to lace their contest entries with magic. So I have gone to several of these shows as a 'fill-in judge' in search of these individuals."

"But why did that mean you had to disrupt the festival?" Ida asked. "I don't see why you couldn't just investigate the people. Why'd you have to destroy Merv's blanket and tip over the pie table and release the livestock?"

"Because his pig is a magical detector," Bev said, finally putting the pieces together. "Isn't he?"

"You seem to know plenty about magical creatures, Bev," Renault said.

"I've unfortunately had my share of interactions with them lately," Bev replied dryly.

"Yes, my *pig,* as you call him, is really a guillen. And while your laelaps can detect magic by scent, unfortunately, mine must do so by taste." He glanced at the dog by Bev's feet. "And as I said, dogs don't like me very much, so I have what I have."

As if on cue, Biscuit growled at him.

"You took my garden to that thicket to let your guillen eat it," Bev said. "Did you…did it eat my entire rosemary plant?"

"I had no choice. The results kept coming back *inconclusive*," he replied with narrowing eyes. "I have to say, I'm still unconvinced you aren't the magic person I was sent to find. But whatever charm you have on yourself…"

"There's no such charm," Bev said with a chuckle. "And you dug up my garden yourself and found nothing, right?"

It was a dare, a question. Bev had to school her features so she didn't give away her own curiosity about the amulet piece.

"Nothing but very well-maintained herbs," he said, almost sadly.

So maybe the amulet isn't *magical?*

"But why did you tip over the pie table?" Ida asked.

"Because one of the pies had barus magic in it," Bev said. "So *you* tipped over the table so they'd all go in the trash, and you could test them without being noticed. And you stole Merv's blanket, too." Bev shook her head, glancing down at Biscuit. "Sorry, boy. Didn't mean to blame you."

Biscuit sniffed.

"And you asked me to bring you to Merv's house," Bev said. "Why?"

"Many times, these powerful magic people will send proxies in their stead," he said. "The pig tasted magic in the yarn, so I wanted to meet the man responsible. But the mole man is simply that. Nothing exciting."

"Then you went to Felicia's after I'd told you Biscuit had been into her things," Bev continued with a nod. "*You're* the one who took her bauble."

"I was surprised she caused such a stink, considering that magic is *highly* illegal." He glanced at Twinsly. "Though I suspect the mayor had something to do with it. She had, well, not magic in her veins, but traces of it all over her clothes."

"*Hah!*" Hendry barked. "I *knew* she was cheating!"

"But why did you release all the livestock?" Ida pressed. "What possible reason—"

"He needed the town empty to search for more magic," Bev said. "He's the one who suggested we get everyone up and searching the countryside. And I bet..." She paused. "How *did* you get all the animals spread out so far?"

"One of the perks of being in Her Majesty's service is that *I* am allowed to conduct a little magic to finish my business," he said. "A small spell here and there is acceptable."

"Which is also how the livestock got out again," Bev said. "Leaving you free to look into each of the gourds."

"It was...unfortunately, my last chance. I hate to return to Queen's Capital and tell Her Majesty I was unable to locate the person in question. But what brought me here were mere rumors and whispers, so perhaps, like all things in this part of the world, the truth is a bit more mundane than the tale."

He walked up to the satchel and picked it up, putting it around his shoulder.

"My guillen's collar is...?"

"In my kitchen," Bev said. "Help yourself."

"Much obliged." He walked toward the front door.

"Is that…it?" Hendry exclaimed. "You ruined our festival and…walk away into the sunset?" She turned to Petula. "And there's nothing to be done about it?"

Petula had been quiet during the entire revelation, but finally lifted her chin and spoke very clearly. "It's obvious to me that there's been external meddling in this festival," she said. "I will be submitting a *full* report to Her Majesty detailing the havoc her servant has wreaked this week. I firmly believe she will be incensed and demand a full inquiry into what happened."

Bev had serious doubts about that, especially after the mess Karolina Hunter and her team had caused.

"But the festival?" Hendry pressed. "Surely… surely we should be given another chance."

Petula was silent for a long time, and no one spoke until she did.

"Since it seems that the chaos *wasn't* the fault of the town," Petula said, "I suppose it can continue this year…"

There was a collective intake of breath as Hendry asked, "And next year?"

Another long, agonizing pause. "*Fine.* The festival can stay in Pigsend."

The entire room erupted in loud, raucous cheers. Ida dove into Vellora's arms, spinning her wife around and planting a huge kiss on her lips. Trent and Herman cried and hugged each other then seemed to realize they'd be back in competition with one another and broke apart with matching scowls. The rest of the room celebrated, clapping each other on the back.

Everyone, of course, except the Middleburg delegation.

"This is outrageous," Twinsly said, stepping forward. "So what if it was...well, an outsider? Clearly, the festival is in need of better management. And we can't discount the fact that there's not enough room to house the people who are invited, nor is there enough—"

"I'd say after twenty years, we're doing fine," Hendry said, her smile wide and cheeky. "If you want your own festival, Miranda, I suggest you start one. There's room in the spring for you."

"I plan to appeal this decision," Twinsly said.

"If I were you, Mayor Twinsly, I would be keeping a low profile," Petula said, her nose lifting. "Especially considering the revelations made about you by Mr. Bonding...er...Lank." She sniffed. "Barus baubles are highly illegal. I don't even know how a member of your town would get their hands on one."

Twinsly's cheeks turned pink. "I don't know what you're talking about. If we had some kind of magic, it's not—"

"As it stands, the bauble has been confiscated by Mr. Lank, and he doesn't see the need to elevate the discovery to the proper authorities," she said. "However, rest assured that I will be *investigating* each of Middleburg's entries into tomorrow's contest to ensure that *no* magic is used."

"How?" Twinsly said.

"Ms.... Er, Bev." Petula turned. "Is it true your dog is a magical detector?"

"He is," Bev said. "A laelaps."

"Then perhaps he will assist me in the effort."

Bev rubbed the back of her neck. Biscuit? Helping with the food contest? That was a bit dicey. "If you want to give it a go, I don't have any objections. But he is...well, he's food motivated."

"If he is, indeed, a laelaps, that means you can control him," Petula said. "I suggest you be very intentional about what you're asking him to do."

"That's grossly unfair," Twinsly said, her voice rising with panic. "Because...um..."

"She's in the bread-making competition!" Felicia said.

Petula lifted a shoulder. "With all the tomfoolery going on this past week by *your* delegation, Mayor Twinsly, I think that using Ms.

Bev's dog will even the scales a bit."

Hendry chuckled. "Serves you right."

Petula let out a weary groan, as if the last half-hour had exhausted her completely. "Now, if we've all had our questions answered, I would like to return to the inn and have a few minutes to collect myself."

"Wait a minute!" Herman Monday cried out. "Who won the gourd contest?"

She sighed. "I will have answers for all winners tomorrow, as planned. But for today..." She shook her head. "Today, I have a *very* long report to write."

CHAPTER TWENTY~THREE

"Okay, Mr. Biscuit, listen *very closely*."

Bev stood outside the town hall the next morning. Inside, her freshly baked rosemary bread —that she'd woken up at midnight to start—was being protected by Vellora *and* Allen. Petula hadn't arrived yet, so Bev was taking a few minutes to make sure her laelaps understood his assignment.

"I know you're going to want to eat everything," Bev said. "But you need to manage your impulses. Your *one* job today is to find magic in the food, okay? If there's magic, I want you to *tell* Ms. Banks. Understand? Don't *eat* anything."

Biscuit opened his mouth, his tongue unfurling

as he smiled at her. It certainly didn't *look* like he was listening.

"Don't embarrass me, please," Bev said, straightening. "Now you wait here until Ms. Banks arrives."

She stepped toward the door, expecting him to follow her, but he stayed put.

"Good boy."

Inside, the room was full of delicious smells. Already, the winners for each of the other contests had been awarded. Merv, unfortunately, didn't even get an honorable mention for his blanket, but Trent's pumpkin had won the gourd contest handily. All that was left was the final round of food, so the bread-makers, pie-makers, and jam-makers were seated in rows in the town hall, holding onto their contest entries. Unsurprisingly, the delegation from Middleburg had left in the night, leaving only those from Pigsend and the surrounding areas to compete.

Everyone, unfortunately, except for Stanton Bucko.

"Well, I tell you, I'm *glad* I returned to Middleburg when I did," he said, holding yet another beautiful loaf of sourdough. "Can't tell you how embarrassed I was to hear that Mayor Twinsly was *in any way* implicated in *any* kind of tomfoolery. And to know that there was a member of the queen's service in town? Well, I'm grateful I had business to attend to back home."

Bev sidled up to Allen and Vellora and took possession of her rosemary bread. Unlike her first entry, this one had been crafted to perfection, and the dried rosemary was coming through like a long-lost friend. She hated to use the last of it, especially since her propagated piece still looked mostly dead, but she was determined to submit something.

"You're going to win, I know it," Allen said.

"And if you don't, I'm gonna roll some heads," Vellora replied.

"I don't need to win," Bev said, glancing at Stanton. "Just competing is winning enough."

"That's what a loser says," Vellora barked. "You gotta own it."

As before, Ida walked around and took samples of each bread. Stanton cleaved his own slice for her, and Bev...well, Bev probably should've done the same, but she let Ida pick the slice. There were only four contestants left, including two farmers from between Pigsend and Middleburg. Once the bread went into Rustin's office, Ida told the contestants they could sit down and await the final awards.

"They'll all be revealed together," Ida said. "Once everyone's been adjudicated."

"Why do we have to wait?" Stanton cried.

"Because it's more interesting that way," Ida

replied, giving him a look. "Jam-makers? You're up. Come grab a number from me."

Bev, Allen, and Vellora took her rosemary bread from the table and headed to an empty bench to sit. Bev broke the bread in half and handed it to Allen and Vellora.

"For your assistance in protecting my entry," she said.

"Ahem." Etheldra's voice echoed behind them.

"Etheldra? What in the...What are you doing here?"

"I made a pie, of course," she said. "And I don't see you handing out that delicious rosemary bread and not offering me a piece, right?"

Allen chuckled and broke his in half, handing it to her. She took the piece happily, taking a bite and making a low sound of enjoyment before wandering back to the rest of the pie-makers.

"How long is this going to take, anyway?" Vellora asked.

"If you need to get back to the butcher shop, you're free to go," Bev said.

"Nah, with the festivalgoers leaving town, our orders have dropped." Vellora puffed out her chest. "Besides that, it's nice to see my wife in action. She really does love this stuff."

"Allen?" Bev said, looking to the other side. "Do you need to get back to the bakery?"

"No, um…" His cheeks reddened. "Vicky's in the jam-making contest. She wanted me to be here."

Bev caught sight of Allen's girlfriend in the pews, and the girl waved at him sheepishly.

"So are you two…official yet?" Vellora asked.

"I mean, not officially, no. But maybe? I don't know." He shuffled his feet as he looked at the ground. "Gotta finish paying off my debts before I can even think about…" He coughed. "Well."

"Allen Mackey, don't you dare let me hear you've been stalling asking your best girl out because you're paying *me* back," Bev scolded. "Your mother would come back and haunt me."

He blushed.

Once the jam was collected, the pie-makers were called. Etheldra hadn't been kidding that she was included in the pie contest, but only two others came up to the podium.

"Ida told me Petula had to scrounge up to find the best of Pigsend, because all the Middleburg people withdrew from the contest," Vellora whispered. "Scandal, scandal."

"Be interesting to see how that shakes out next year," Bev said, turning in her seat. "Is Petula even here yet?"

As if summoned, the back doors opened and Petula came strolling into the room, Biscuit walking nicely by her side. Bev almost didn't recognize the dog, he was being so well-behaved. But she absolutely held her breath as Petula sat at the front table, and Biscuit hopped onto the seat next to her.

"Bring me the jams."

Ida brought forth four plates with jam samples on each one. Petula first had Biscuit inspect each one. Bev closed her eyes, praying her laelaps wouldn't gobble everything up. But to her surprise, he sniffed then looked at Petula expectantly as she tasted each one, jotting down notes on a paper.

"Now, the breads."

Vellora and Allen took Bev's hand as the four pieces of bread were placed on the table. Bev could see the flecks of rosemary in her bread and held her breath as Biscuit sniffed hers for a long time. But he didn't react, so Petula took a bite and carried on.

"Finally, the pies."

The same routine followed, and within minutes, Petula was wiping her mouth and counting on her page.

"I would first like to say," she announced, earning something of a groan from the audience, "that this has been the most...memorable festival I've ever attended. It brings me joy to see so many of you so invested in the agricultural arts, and to be so motivated to hold and maintain a festival of this size in your town."

"Oh my goodness, get on with it," Allen

muttered.

But she went on, dragging out the decision as she spoke of the importance of *fairness* and *adherence to rules*. Bev had never once been impatient for anything, but as the minutes ticked on, and the monologue showed no end in sight, she tapped her foot impatiently.

"And so," she said, "it is my pleasure to offer the following awards."

Bev perked up.

"In the category of jam-making, honorable mention, Ms. Mandisa Munson."

Polite applause erupted as a farmer from outside Pigsend hurried up to the front to grab a yellow ribbon. Her face was bright red as she clutched it and carried it back to her seat.

"And in the category of jam-making, first prize, Ms. Mandy Nowak."

Allen immediately turned to Vicky, whose face had fallen in disappointment. Bev nudged him to get up and go to her, and luckily, the dumb kid did something right, putting his arm around his would-be girlfriend as she rested her teary cheek on his shoulder.

"Now, in the category of pie-making, honorable mention…"

Bev blew air between her lips as the honorable mention for pie was given to Gilda Climber, the blacksmith's apprentice, and Etheldra took home the top prize. Her pulse was speeding up as they drew closer and closer to the final award.

"In our final category, bread-making," Petula said. "The honorable mention goes to…"

Vellora's grip on Bev's hand grew so tight she lost blood flow.

"Bev!"

The entire town hall erupted in cheers as Vellora pushed Bev to her feet. She was stunned—her mouth falling open as she stumbled to the front. Biscuit was wagging his tail happily as she approached, and even Petula looked mildly happy to be giving her the ribbon.

"It was very *very* close," she said, under the din of applause. "And perhaps…perhaps I might've been tilted one way to avoid the look of impropriety, considering your dog was… But I want you to know…that is perhaps the *best* rosemary bread I've ever had in my life."

Bev turned, beaming with joy as she walked back to her seat.

"Yes, yes, settle down," Petula said, holding up her hands. "Finally, first prize in bread-making goes to…Stanton Bucko!"

It was relative crickets compared to the cheers Bev got, and she felt a little bad for the Middleburg baker as he rose to accept his award. As soon as he took the ribbon, the crowd erupted in conversation, and Bev was absolutely swamped by well-wishers and congratulators, including Ida, Etheldra, and even Mayor Hendry.

"I knew you could do it," she said, shaking Bev's hand.

"But I didn't win," Bev said.

"You got a ribbon, that's all I care about." She adjusted her tunic. "Now if you'll excuse me, I have a letter to write to Miranda."

Bev could barely keep up with all the conversations around her, and her cheeks threatened to fall off from all the grinning. Finally, the crowd seemed to thin, and Bev stood in the afterglow of the celebrations.

"You did it!" Ida squealed, practically throwing herself onto Bev. "I'm *so* proud of you!"

"I can't believe I won a ribbon!" Bev said, looking at it again. Sure enough, it was embroidered with *Honorable Mention, Bread-Making Contest.* It was the most beautiful thing she'd ever seen.

"Well, it's not a first prize, but it'll do," Stanton said, meandering over wearing his blue ribbon on his chest. "Will we be seeing you next year?"

"I suppose I have to," Bev said with a chuckle. "And you?"

"If I'm allowed back, I plan to continue my streak." He held out his hand. "I do have to know, if your garden was destroyed, where did you get the rosemary?"

"Turns out my friends had stashed some away." Bev grinned to Ida, who seemed to be dying to ask Stanton if the stalk she'd found in his room had been clipped from her bush, but it didn't seem important now. "Hoping that the sprig I planted will propagate now, or I'm going to have to start all over. Luckily, I was able to find the rest of my garden and salvage that, so I won't be without my herbs this winter."

"What, erm...do you think it is about your rosemary that makes it taste so good?" Stanton asked.

"It's not magic, I can assure you of that," Bev said. "Claude or Renault or whatever his name is was clear in his diary that his pig ate the entire plant and found nothing."

"Inconclusive, I think, was the phrase I heard," Stanton said with a look.

"Well, if there's magic, it's not mine," Bev said. "I guess it'll have to remain a mystery."

~

Bev was on cloud nine the rest of the day, humming through her chores and proudly displaying her ribbon for all to see during a very small but boisterous dinner that night. It was all her regular patrons, plus Ida, Vellora, Vicky, and Allen, who'd baked a cake for all to enjoy. Even Biscuit got into the mix, eating several slices of cake and beef before falling asleep in front of the fire.

And if that weren't enough, everyone who came to dinner helped her clean, so the inn was spick-and-span within an hour.

With the inn empty of travelers for the first time in a week, Bev retreated to her room early with her prize and dog. Biscuit curled up in a ball on her bed and continued his snooze while Bev admired the ribbon in all its beautiful detail. She was placing it on her windowsill next to the small rosemary plant when she stopped short.

"Is that…?"

A grin blossomed on her face. *Her rosemary plant had sprung a new branch!*

It was alive!

She could've kissed it but didn't want to break any of the branches. So she settled for a little happy dance before changing into her night clothes and crawling into bed. Before long, she and Biscuit were fast asleep.

But not for long—because something was glowing.

Bev sat up, groggy. It was certainly not time to wake up. Biscuit growled as she sat up and searched her room for the source of the glow.

"What in the…"

She opened the top drawer and pulled out the illuminated amulet fragment. As she held it, magic sizzled at her fingertips, almost causing her to toss the thing back into her drawer.

She jumped when Biscuit placed his paws on her thighs, but surprise turned into curiosity as the dog —laelaps—sniffed the amulet like it was something *very* interesting to him.

Still, as Bev stared at it, she couldn't help but feel it was time to get rid of the blasted thing. It had already nearly cost her a garden, and before that, her inn. Having it on her person was asking for trouble, especially since the queen's people seemed to know something was afoot in Pigsend.

"Okay, B," Bev said. "Let's go for a walk."

Although it was very late, Bev didn't want to chance being seen by anyone, so she headed toward the forest thicket that Biscuit seemed excited about. She reasoned that if someone had found it there, she could simply blame it on Claude/Renault and say it must've been his, considering his pig had been so infatuated with the area.

For what she hoped was the last time, she made her way through the brambles and branches until she reached the clearing. She couldn't chuck it anywhere—she'd have to make sure it was hidden enough that someone passing by wouldn't see it.

Biscuit was sniffing the ground in the corner—the same place she'd found Merv's blanket, so Bev assumed it would be more yarn, but he began digging in the dirt. There was something... something in the ground. Glowing, like the amulet piece.

She knelt beside him, reaching into the thicket and pulled out...another piece of the amulet.

"Oh...no..." Bev looked around. One piece was bad enough. Two? That was absolutely asking for...

She was standing in a field covered in blood. Everything was red, including her hands. The sound of dying soldiers echoed around her, as did the stench of...

Bev snapped back into herself, shivering as the memory flitted through her consciousness.

"Absolutely not."

She chucked the amulet back into the hole where Biscuit had found it then took the other and flung it as far as it would go into the thicket.

Whatever memories wanted to come to the surface could stay buried and if the queen's people found the amulet, oh well. *She* wasn't getting pulled into this nonsense—whatever had happened in the past was better left there.

"Let's go, B."

Bev continues her adventures in

SECRETS AND SNOWFLAKES

Weary Dragon Inn

BOOK THREE

Acknowlegments

Oh, what a lovely, fun ride this was, start-to-finish. I wrote it while on pregnancy bedrest in January 2023, and let me tell you, Bev was exactly the book I needed to write at that time. I wrote 61,000 words in 16 days so… I clearly was in need of escape.

My most heartfelt thanks goes to my husband, who continues to be my strongest supporter and solid rock as we continue our adventure as partners and parents. Thank you to my parents, Aunt Louise, Aunt Red, and my in-laws for stepping up during our season of chaos to help out with the toddler so I could focus on…well, this.

My MI(L)F Discord writing group continued to be my sounding board and sanity check, as well as my beta readers, Chelsea and Ybelline. Of course, thanks to Danielle Fine, my amazing editor, and Lisa Henson, my incredible final proofer.

Finally, in case it wasn't obvious, Mr. Biscuit was my beloved, mischievous beagle-chihuahua rescue dog that held a piece of my heart for over ten years. Having to say goodbye to him was the hardest thing I've ever done, but writing him into Bev's adventures was healing and made me remember the good (and not-so-well-behaved) times. I'm grateful I was able to memorialize him in this way.

KICKSTARTER BACKERS

Finally, thanks go to the Kickstarter backers, who not only wanted to get the *first* Bev book, but were so eager to hear her story that they bought book two as well.

Aaron Frost, Aaron Jamieson, Abby Brew, Abigail Conner, Abra Roth, Adam Cole, Adam Kerstin, Adrianne Carley, AingealWroth, Alaska Momster, Alessandro Colombo, Alexandra Fluskey, Allison Torres, Alyssa Emmert, Amanda Gerdel, Amy Chadwick, André Laude, Andrew Kaplan, Andy, Anil Kadam, Ann Cofell, Anna, Anonymous, aoife & ryan, Archibald Nastyface Hethrenton, Aruhi, Ashley Matics, Ashley Stark, Becca Stillo, Becky B, Becky Carr, Becky James, Bethany Pratt, Bettina Pickett, Blake Strickland, Blumpsie, Boris Veytsman, Bree, Brett Werst, Brian Bauer, Bridget Horn, Bridgette Findley, Brock Miller, C. A. Maxwell, Caitlyn M Nye, Caitlyn Miller, Camilla Vavruch, Carlos Guerra, Carly Occhifinto, Catherine Sampson, CAVE321, Chase Sanders, Chelsea, Chris A McGee, Chris King, Chris Ward, Christa Rumage, Christa S. Rickard, Christian Holt, Christiana Laudie, Christine Crew, Clarissa Gosling, Cody L. Allen, Colin Letch, Conor, Cullen 'Towelman' Gilchrist, Dale A Russell, Danielle Perry, Dave and Rose Fonville, Dave Baughman, Dave Luxton, Dave Marchetti, David Haskins, David Holzborn, David

Lewis, Day Leitao, Dead Fishie, DeeAnna, Dexter Jacobs, Doris Wooding, Douglas & Nicole Williams, Drea Laj, Dustin Thatcher, E. Snelgrove, E.M. Middel, E.V. Everest, E.V. Green, Eddie Joo, Edward E., Elise Roberts, Elizabeth F, Elle Wilson, Ellen Pilcher, Emily Gibbs, Emma Cohan, Emma S, Erica Blumenthal, Erika Jo, Eva Ali, Felicia, Gary Olsen, GhostCat, Gina Lucas, Gina Points, Ginny L., Golinssohn, Grace Parsons, Greg Rice, Greg Tausch, Gretchen, Hana Correa, Hannah, Heather A. McBride, His & Hearse Press, Hollow Mask, Hollysbookadventure, Howard Blakeslee, Isabel Johnson, J R Forst, J Truscott, Jan Birch, Jan Dierker, Janelle Boys-Chen, Jean Sitkei, Jeffrey M. Johnson, Jennifer, Jennifer Brown, Jennifer Eaton, Jennifer Katsch, Jeremy S, Jesi Blair, Jessi Pike, Jessica Guyette, Jessica Stanton, Joe G, Joe Monson, Joel silvey, John Idlor, John Markley, Johnathan Detrick, Jolene Pierce, Jonathan Snavely, Josh Samples, Joshua, Julia Byers, KA Ramadorai, Kanyon Kiernan, Karen Fonville, Karen Low, Karen Scharff, Karen Tankersley, Karley Rech, Kat Brady, Kat James, Kate Ehrenholm, Katie, Katie L. Carroll, Katie VanWyhe, Katrina Drake, Kaycee Castleman, Keelyn Wright, Keli, Kelsey Hunt, Kenneth Brown, Kiera Storch, Kourtney & William Stauffer, Krissy Pallen, Kristen & Eric Terlep, Kristian Handberg, Kristin Paine Wallin, KRR Lockhaven, Krysti Matheson, Kurt Beyerl, Lacey Holloway, Larry Couch, Laura L Nelson, Lauren Kildea, Leslie Twitchell, Lindachelle, Lindsey Ferebee, Lindsey Thurman, Lisa Henson, Liz Jordan, Lorin Jones, Luke Italiano, M. H. Woodscourt, Marc D Long, Marcus U, Marilyn Donahue, Marine Lesne, Mark T.

Eckstein, Marte Myrvold, Matthian, MC, Meghan DiMarco, Melanie Pokroy, Melissa, Melissa C, Michael B Mitchell, Michael J. Sullivan, author, Michał Kabza, Michelle E. LaCrosse, Molly J Stanton, Nathaniel Webb, Nicole wagner, Niels-Peter, Nikita Johnson, None, Noreen Gwilliam, Oliver Gross, OwainB, Patricia Miller, Patrick Moore, Paul, peter jockel, Phil Beneker, pjk, Polina "Polinchka" Bazlova, prefer not to be named :), R.J. Marchetti, Rachel S., Rachel Stoddard, Rafi Spitzer, Ramón Terrell, Raphael Bressel, Ray Lorenz, Raymond B, Rebecca, Rebecca Buchanan, René Schultze, Renee, Richard Deltoro, Richard Novak, Richard Sayer, Risa Scranton, Rob Steinberger, Robert K. Barbour, Robert Sanders, Robert Stuart, Roman Pauer, Rowan Stone, Russell Ventimeglia, Ryan C., Ryan Scott James, Samantha Eckiss, Samantha Landstrom, Sandy Garza, Sarah, Sarah B, Sarah L. Stevenson, Scantrontb, Scott Casey, Scott Walker, Sean Bradley, Sebastian Ernst, Señor Neo, Serena M, Seth Alexander, Shadowfall, Shaelei, Sierra Davenport, Sissel K. H. Rasmussen, sonoghen, Sophia, Stefke Leuhery, Stephanie Bailey, Stephanie Horn, Stephanie Webb, Stephany, Stephen, Stephen Kotowych, Steve Locke, Steve Untch, Susan Buescher, Suzann P, Taylor Winsor, Terri Connor, Terry, Terry Evans, Momma, Tessa, TF Drifter, The Calderon-Medina family, The Creative Fund by BackerKit, The Freeman Family, Theresa Snyder, Tom Dean, Tony, Tracy Popey, V G Murray, Valerie Bolster, William J. Robbins, Wineke Sloos, xellos, Yngve J. K. Hestem, Zero

ALSO BY THE AUTHOR

The Princess Vigilante Series

Brynna has been protecting her kingdom as a masked vigilante until one night, she's captured by the king's guards. Instead of arresting her, the captain tells her that her father and brother have been assassinated and she must hang up her mask and become queen.

The Princess Vigilante series is a four-book young adult epic fantasy series, perfect for fans of Throne of Glass and Graceling.

THE SEOD CROÍ CHRONICLES

After her father's murder, princess Ayla is set to take the throne — but to succeed, she needs the magical stone her evil stepmother stole. Fortunately, wizard apprentice Cade and knight Ward are both eager to win Ayla's favor.

A Quest of Blood and Stone is the first book in the *Seod Croí* chronicles and is available now in eBook, paperback, and hardcover.

Also By the Author

The Madion War Trilogy

He's a prince, she's a pilot, they're at war. But when they are marooned on a deserted island hundreds of miles from either nation, they must set aside their differences and work together if they want to survive.

The Madion War Trilogy is a fantasy romance available now in eBook, Paperback, and Hardcover.

empath

Lauren Dailey is in break-up hell, but if you ask her she's doing just great. She hears a mysterious voice promising an easy escape from her problems and finds herself in a brand new world where she has the power to feel what others are feeling. Just one problem—there's a dragon in the mountains that happens to eat Empaths. And it might be the source of the mysterious voice tempting her deeper into her own darkness.

Empath is a stand-alone fantasy that is available now in eBook, Paperback, and Hardcover.

About the Author

S. Usher Evans was born and raised in Pensacola, Florida. After a decade of fighting bureaucratic battles as an IT consultant in Washington, DC, she suffered a massive quarter-life-crisis. She found fighting dragons was more fun than writing policy, so she moved back to Pensacola to write books full-time. She currently resides there with her husband and kids, and frequently can be found plotting on the beach.

Visit S. Usher Evans online at:
http://www.susherevans.com/

Milton Keynes UK
Ingram Content Group UK Ltd.
UKHW021932181023
430887UK00013B/105/J

9 781945 438608